Gallery Books
Editor Peter Fallon

HEDDA GABLER

Brian Friel

HEDDA GABLER

after Ibsen

Gallery Books

Hedda Gabler
was first published
simultaneously in paperback
and in a clothbound edition
on the day of its première
30 September 2008.

The Gallery Press
Loughcrew
Oldcastle
County Meath
Ireland

© Brian Friel 2008

ISBN   978 1 85235 457 2 *paperback*
       978 1 85235 458 9 *clothbound*

A CIP catalogue record for this book
is available from the British Library.

Characters

HEDDA GABLER (29), daughter of General Gabler and George
    Tesman's wife
GEORGE TESMAN (33), research graduate in cultural history
JULIANA TESMAN (65), George's aunt
BERTHA (60), Juliana's maid
EILERT LOEVBORG (33), writer and sociologist
THEA ELVSTED (26), wife of a resident magistrate
JUDGE BRACK (45)

Place

The Tesman house in a fashionable part of the city.

Time

The year 1890.

　　Act One — early morning in September.
　　Act Two — that afternoon.
　　Act Three — dawn, the following day.
　　Act Four — that evening.

Set

A large drawing room decorated in dark colours and carefully furnished — a round table, chairs, an armchair, a footstool, a porcelain stove, an upright piano.

In the left hand wall (left and right from the point of view of the audience) a door leads to the hall. In the right hand wall a French window with the curtains pulled back. Through this window we see part of a verandah and autumn trees.

In the back wall of the drawing room a wide doorway with its curtains pulled back. Through it we see a smaller room with decor and furnishings similar to the drawing room — round table, sofa, chairs, terracotta ornaments. Clearly visible on a wall in this smaller room is a large portrait of an elderly General Gabler, Hedda's father, resplendent and formidable in full military uniform.

There are several bunches of fresh flowers on the drawing-room table, on top of the piano and in vases around both rooms.

Hedda Gabler was first performed in the Gate Theatre, Dublin, as part of the Dublin Theatre Festival, on Tuesday, 30 September 2008, with the following cast:

HEDDA GABLER	Justine Mitchell
GEORGE TESMAN	Peter Hanly
JULIANA TESMAN	Susan FitzGerald
BERTHA	Billie Traynor
EILERT LOEVBORG	John Light
THEA ELVSTED	Andrea Irvine
JUDGE BRACK	Andrew Woodall
Director	Anna Mackmin
Designer	Lez Brotherston
Lighting designer	Oliver Fenwick
Music	Denis Clohessy

for Cassandra Fusco

ACT ONE

JULIANA TESMAN *comes in from the hall. She is a pleasant, kindly spinster in her mid-sixties. In outdoor clothes, wearing a hat, carrying a parasol. She pauses and looks round the silent drawing room.*

JULIANA   (*Softly to herself*) I was afraid of that.
BERTHA   (*Off*) What's that, Miss?
JULIANA   Shhhh!

> BERTHA *enters. She is a few years younger than* JULIANA. *She is carrying a bunch of flowers.*

BERTHA   What did you say, Miss Juliana?
JULIANA   Keep your voice down, Bertha. We're too early. They're not up yet.
BERTHA   He must be exhausted.
JULIANA   They both must be exhausted.
BERTHA   Why wouldn't he be? It was all hours before the steamer berthed. And then, when she got up here, nothing would do her but she'd unpack everything *before* she went to bed.
JULIANA   She's a very efficient young woman.
BERTHA   Why does she call me Berna then?
JULIANA   She just misheard your name.
BERTHA   Huh! She must have had a dozen trunks of stuff.
JULIANA   Four, Bertha; just four.
BERTHA   And nine boxes — I counted them.
JULIANA   (*Ironically*) Good for you.

> JULIANA *throws open the French windows.*

Well, let them have a good lie in. And put those flowers down somewhere.

11

BERTHA Where?

JULIANA There — anywhere. And when they do come down they can fill their lungs with good Norwegian air.

BERTHA Where will I put — ?

JULIANA Give them to me.

> JULIANA *takes the flowers brusquely out of* BERTHA*'s hand and puts them on top of the piano.*

BERTHA I'm never going to get the hang of this house, Miss Juliana.

JULIANA Don't be silly.

BERTHA (*Close to tears*) It's not going to work out. I know it's not. And I'm afraid —

> JULIANA *puts her arms around her.*

JULIANA We'll have none of that, Bertha. You're going to be very happy here. Do you think I would have parted with you to anybody but Miss Hedda? And you'll have George, won't you? — our darling Georgie that you have taken care of since he was a baby. But what am *I* going to do without *you*?

BERTHA You're the only family I've every known, you and Master George and lovely Miss Rena.

JULIANA Very little will change. You'll just carry on looking after George in this house as you've always done all your life — and Mrs George, too, of course. And I'll drop in as often as I can.

BERTHA But that new maid you've got, she won't be able to look after Miss Rena. A big, rough lump like that, she wouldn't know how to handle an invalid.

JULIANA She'll learn, Berna.

BERTHA (*Cautioning*) Miss!

JULIANA Sorry. And I'll be there. We'll manage.

BERTHA And Miss Hedda — Mrs George — I just know she doesn't like me.

JULIANA (*Wearily*) 'Doesn't like — ' What nonsense is that! She scarcely knows you yet.

BERTHA She's a cold woman.

JULIANA And when you get to know each other you'll grow to love her — and not only because she's George's wife.

BERTHA And a very bossy woman.

JULIANA She's a determined young woman, yes. Isn't she the daughter of General Gabler? And brought up with a household of orderlies to boss around? Remember, we used to see her out riding with her father on an enormous black horse; in this elegant black riding dress?

BERTHA And a feather in her hat, kind of defiant. Who would have thought that herself and our Georgie would ever have made a — ?

JULIANA Not simply 'our Georgie' any more, Bertha. They made him a doctor when he was away in Germany. Our Georgie is now Doctor George Tesman.

BERTHA I know.

JULIANA And he is *so* thrilled by it: blurted it out last night before we were at the foot of the gangway. (*Realizing*) How did you know?

BERTHA It was her first instruction when she stepped into this house. 'From now on you'll address Mr Tesman as Doctor Tesman.'

JULIANA Imagine if poor Joachim had lived to see his precious little boy grow into such an accomplished man. And there may be an even more important title coming his way soon.

BERTHA Bigger than Doctor?

JULIANA Bigger than Doctor.

BERTHA What would be bigger than Doctor?

JULIANA Guess.

BERTHA They're going to make a vet out of him!

JULIANA He's not that kind of doctor, Bertha. He's an academic doctor. But when the other title comes along, as he would say himself, 'My goodness. Oh my goodness.' Anyhow . . . Why did you take the loose covers off the chairs?

BERTHA She told me to — Miss Hedda. They remind her of

shrouds, she said.

JULIANA So they must be going to make this their living room then.

GEORGE TESMAN *enters from the back room. He is thirty-three, genial, open, very enthusiastic.* JUDGE BRACK *describes him as 'decent, credulous, trusting' — in other words he can be simultaneously admirable and infuriating. He is carrying an empty suitcase.*

Good morning, George.

GEORGE Auntie Juju! (*He embraces her excitedly*) Well, isn't this a wonderful surprise first thing in the morning!

JULIANA I'm afraid it *is* a bit early to —

GEORGE Early? Not a bit! The earlier the better! And Bertha! (*He embraces her with equal enthusiasm*) How are you, Bertha?

JULIANA She hasn't slept for three nights waiting for you to come home.

BERTHA It was the toothache really.

GEORGE My very own Bertha! Look at the two of you! My goodness. Oh my goodness. I'm so glad to see you both. What a great joy to come down to this! And thank you for meeting us off the tender last night. That wasn't at all necessary.

JULIANA I just dropped by to see that you're settled in.

GEORGE As if we had lived here all our lives. We were so sorry we couldn't squeeze you into the carriage last night, Auntie Juju. But there was scarcely room for me with all darling Hedda's luggage.

BERTHA A dozen trunks and nine boxes.

GEORGE At least, Bertha! How did you get home?

JULIANA Judge Brack saw me right up to my door.

GEORGE Good for him. Well, what an unqualified joy to come down to this! As if I'd never left home! All we need now is lovely Auntie Rena and we'd be a complete family again. How is she?

JULIANA I'm afraid my darling sister is slipping away slowly and very quietly.

GEORGE Oh, Auntie Juju.

JULIANA It's not easy to watch.

GEORGE Must be awful.

JULIANA I really think Bertha keeps her alive.

BERTHA I wish I could.

GEORGE I'm sure that's true.

JULIANA You'll see a big change.

GEORGE I'll go over today.

JULIANA But if she weren't there — and now with you gone — my life would be hollow — wouldn't it?

GEORGE I'm not gone, Auntie Juju! I'm very much here! (*She kisses his cheek*) And I'll always be here!

BERTHA Is there anything I can do for Miss Hedda?

GEORGE Not a thing, Bertha, thank you. We'll let her sleep a little longer. You can do something for me, though: put this (*case*) in the attic, would you?

BERTHA Certainly, 'Doctor'.

GEORGE 'Doctor'! Is Miss Bertha being saucy with me?

BERTHA (*Coyly, as she exits*) And maybe a vet soon!

GEORGE (*Puzzled*) Vet?

JULIANA We are all so very proud of you, Georgie.

GEORGE And isn't it a shocking thing to admit — no, not shocking, embarrassing, no, not embarrassing, pathetic, really pathetic — I'm very proud of myself! You saw that case? Packed with the material for my new book. You wouldn't believe what I unearthed all over Europe — in archives, museums, private libraries — stuff people had completely forgotten was there. Absolutely incredible material!

JULIANA So your honeymoon wasn't all gadding about and pleasure then?

GEORGE Certainly not! And I want another hug! (*He hugs her*) Sit down beside me before Hedda appears and tell me all the gossip I've missed in the past six months. Here, take your hat off. No, that was always my job, wasn't it?

He slowly removes her hat.

JULIANA It's just as if you were still home with us.

GEORGE It's new, isn't it?

JULIANA A week old. Got it in a charity sale.

GEORGE Well, if Miss Juliana Tesman isn't the most elegant lady in town.

JULIANA I got it for Hedda — so that she won't be ashamed of me if we were to go for a walk together.

He hugs her again quickly.

GEORGE You are a very special — a most special aunt.

JULIANA I think your honeymoon was the longest six months of my life. There were times when I wondered would I ever see you again!

GEORGE Here I am!

JULIANA And a married man! I have to keep telling myself: our Georgie is married to Hedda Gabler that half the men in town were mad about.

GEORGE I know. Lucky, lucky George Tesman.

JULIANA Indeed.

GEORGE More than lucky. Blessed. I'm blessed — amn't I?

JULIANA You deserve to be. But my secret hope is that you have great good news for me. Well?

GEORGE I gave you all my news in my letters.

JULIANA *Really* good news.

GEORGE Getting the doctorate? But I told you all that —

JULIANA No, no, no, no — *great* good news — you know, you and Hedda — special news, Georgie.

GEORGE The professorship?

JULIANA That's not quite what —

GEORGE As good as mine, Auntie Juju, if you believe the rumours.

JULIANA Ah.

GEORGE The appointment will be announced very soon. Professor George Tesman — hasn't it a ring to it?

JULIANA Yes.

GEORGE So I'll be doubly blessed, won't I?

JULIANA I hope so. That long honeymoon must have cost you a fortune, George?

GEORGE	Several fortunes.
JULIANA	(*Anxiously*) It didn't, did it?
GEORGE	Joking — joking. Yes, it was expensive: my wife isn't exactly a frugal woman. But the grant covered most of — well, some of it. Don't worry. Everything is in hand.
JULIANA	Have you had a chance to look over the house yet?
GEORGE	I was up at daybreak.
JULIANA	Well?
GEORGE	The house is wonderful. The house is magnificent.
JULIANA	It's a beautiful home.
GEORGE	But what are we to do with the two extra rooms between the back door and Hedda's bedroom?
JULIANA	(*Coyly*) Oh, you'll find a use for them — in time, George.
GEORGE	For my library! The very thing!
JULIANA	Yes, for your library.
GEORGE	Good idea, Auntie Juju. Yes, we were so lucky to get it. The only house in town Hedda always said she'd ever live in and it comes on the market as we're setting off on our honeymoon. And what do the cautious Tesmans do? Promptly buy it!
JULIANA	But a very dear house.
GEORGE	These things are all relative, aren't they? Anyhow Judge Brack got us very favourable terms. He wrote to Hedda and explained it all.
JULIANA	And I've gone security for the rugs and these bits and pieces.
GEORGE	You?
JULIANA	Why the surprise?
GEORGE	Darling Auntie Juju, you have no money.
JULIANA	Darling nephew Georgie, I have my annuity, haven't I?
GEORGE	But your annuity is the only —
JULIANA	So I raised a modest mortgage on Aunt Rena's and my trust fund.
GEORGE	But that's the only money you've got in the whole world!
JULIANA	No risk involved. A mere formality, Judge Brack

assures me. And to be able to help you in any small way I can — don't you know how much pleasure that gives *me*? No father, no mother, just two ancient aunts to give you a little assistance. And look at how wonderfully you've turned out! You're a very successful young man, Dr Tesman.

GEORGE   Am I?

JULIANA   'Am I?' A magnificent home.

GEORGE   An adorable aunt.

JULIANA   A beautiful wife.

GEORGE   Two adorable aunts.

JULIANA   A well deserved doctorate.

GEORGE   Indeed.

JULIANA   A professorship just round the corner.

GEORGE   Yes! The question is: will George Tesman ever come down to earth again?

JULIANA   Don't be in a hurry. And where are all those rivals of yours now? All those mean-spirited contemporaries who tried to thwart every move you made? Washed up! And that most unfortunate wretch of them all, that awful libertine who seemed to overshadow everything you ever accomplished, where is *he* now?

GEORGE   (*Laughs*) 'Libertine'! The lady can't be talking about my very old friend, Eilert Loevborg, can she?

JULIANA   Friend!

GEORGE   The hugely talented Eilert Loevborg?

JULIANA   Debauchee!

GEORGE   She may be, I suspect.

JULIANA   Lying in some squalid bed of his own making — I hope.

GEORGE   (*Pretended shock*) Auntie Juju!

JULIANA   God forgive me.

GEORGE   Yes, indeed. Have you heard anything about Loevborg in the past six months?

JULIANA   Just that he has brought out a new book.

GEORGE   (*Very shocked*) He has not!

JULIANA   For what it's worth.

GEORGE   Eilert Loevborg — well, isn't he astonishing! A new book!

JULIANA If anybody's interested.
GEORGE Oh, people are very interested, Auntie Juju.
JULIANA Now when your book comes out, then they'll sit up.

BERTHA *returns.*

What's it about, George?
BERTHA You shouldn't leave Miss Rena alone for too long.
JULIANA Going in a moment.
GEORGE Domestic craft and husbandry as practised in Holland and parts of Belgium in the tenth century.
JULIANA Fascinating.
GEORGE You're very sweet. It won't appear for a very long time. There are months of research and cataloguing to be done.
JULIANA And you're good at that. But when it does appear!
BERTHA Miss Juliana . . .
JULIANA I know — I know — I'm going, Bertha.
GEORGE Can't wait to get at it. And in my own home.
JULIANA And with the woman of your dreams.
GEORGE That's the most wonderful thing ever happened to me, Juju.
JULIANA I know.
GEORGE Can't get over Loevborg having a new book out. Ah, Hedda!

HEDDA *enters the back room. Good height, striking appearance, aristocratic face, cold, grey eyes. Dressed in an elegant dressing gown.*

JULIANA Good morning, dear Hedda; a very good morning.
HEDDA Good morning to you, Miss Tesman. (*To* BERTHA) Don't you know where the kitchen is? (*To* JULIANA) An early visit, isn't it?
GEORGE (*To* BERTHA, *as she exits*) Thank you.
BERTHA What's that?
GEORGE For leaving up my case.
JULIANA I know; far too early. I've already apologized to George. And did you sleep well in your new home?

HEDDA Off and on.

GEORGE 'Off and — '! You were out cold when I got up.

HEDDA New surroundings take a little getting used to, Miss Tesman.

JULIANA Juliana — Julia — even Juju, I'm afraid.

HEDDA So it will take some time. (*Sharply*) Why did the maid open those windows? That sun is blinding.

JULIANA I'll close them.

HEDDA George, you close them. No, just pull the curtains. The atmosphere's stifling with all those flowers.

GEORGE *pulls the curtains.*

GEORGE There you are. Fresh air *and* shade.

HEDDA Aren't you going to sit down, Miss Tesman?

JULIANA I've got to get back, thank you — now that I know you're both fine. If I'm away for any length of time poor Rena gets so agitated.

GEORGE Give her my love.

JULIANA I will.

GEORGE And tell her I'll be over to see her this afternoon.

JULIANA Oh, George! I almost forgot! For you.

From her bag she produces a package wrapped in paper.

GEORGE Yes?

JULIANA From Rena.

HEDDA *busies herself taking flowers from the top of the piano and arranging them in vases on the floor.*

GEORGE (*Opening parcel*) Oh, for heaven's sake, I don't believe it! Would you look at that! Look, Hedda, look! My slippers!

HEDDA (*She does not look*) 'For heaven's sake.'

GEORGE (*To* JULIANA) She knows all about them. (*He kisses them. To* HEDDA) Aren't they magnificent?

HEDDA From the moment he realized he'd left them behind

the honeymoon was a disaster.

GEORGE That's unfair. But yes — yes — yes — they are very important to me. Look, Hedda — Auntie Rena's exquisite embroidery. I told you about it. Every year, as soon as my birthday came around, she would painstakingly sketch out a new wild flower and then embroider it. It might take two — three — months to finish it. There's a wake-robin. And a sea aster. And that was for my twenty-fifth — that triumphant *Cardamine pratensis* — that's a lady's smock. Look at the subtlety, the precision, of those lilac leaves. And an autumn crocus. And a shepherd's purse. All those shy greens and browns and cheeky pinks. And a white archangel. And a saucy little vetch for my eighteenth. Such skill — such artistry. Oh my goodness. This is a chronicle of my life, Hedda; a record of my deepest emotions, my most opulent memories. Look, Hedda.

HEDDA What has it to do with me?

GEORGE What do you — ?

HEDDA Not my emotions, not my memories, are they?

GEORGE No, they're not, darling. But if they're —

JULIANA Hedda's right, George. They are very special — to you.

GEORGE But Hedda's part of the family now and surely what is important to —

HEDDA We've got to let that maid go, Miss Tesman.

JULIANA Bertha?!

GEORGE Let Bertha go?

JULIANA Oh, Hedda . . .

GEORGE What are you saying, Hedda?

HEDDA What sort of a sloven is she? Things lying all over the place. Flowers scattered everywhere. Look at that old hat lying here on a chair.

GEORGE (*Gently*) That's Auntie Juju's old hat, Hedda.

HEDDA Ah?

JULIANA And it's a relatively young hat.

HEDDA (*Shrugs*) My mistake.

JULIANA In fact this is its first outing on *my* head.

GEORGE   And what a very, very blessed hat it is to be worn by such an elegant —

JULIANA   Don't be silly, George: hats can't be blessed — only people. (*Holds out her hand*) My parasol if you please. Mine also, Hedda; and *brand* new.

GEORGE   I've never seen you look more graceful, Auntie Juju. (*To* HEDDA) Isn't she graceful?

HEDDA   Lovely.

GEORGE   And you're lovely, too, Hedda. Beautiful. Beautiful without qualification. (*To* JULIANA) Isn't Hedda beautiful?

JULIANA   Hedda has always been beautiful.

JULIANA moves towards the door.

GEORGE   And filled out a little on our travels, hasn't she? Just a little more ample? Attractively more ample?

HEDDA   (*Sharply*) George, please.

JULIANA stops and turns back.

GEORGE   She thinks that dressing gown disguises it but I can tell you —

HEDDA   You can tell nothing at all.

GEORGE   I can, you know, I can! Of course all those enormous plates of fruit strudel we devoured in the Tyrol, they all contributed as well.

HEDDA   I'm exactly the same as I was before we went away.

GEORGE   Sorry, my darling. Just that tiny bit plumper and hugely more attractive.

HEDDA   Oh for God's sake!

GEORGE   Amn't I right, Auntie Juju?

JULIANA looks at HEDDA for a few seconds.

JULIANA   Hedda is beautiful. Hedda is just so beautiful.

Now she goes to HEDDA, takes her head between her hands, draws it towards her, and kisses her on the forehead.

God bless you and keep you, Hedda Tesman. For George's sake.

HEDDA breaks away.

HEDDA   Please — please —
JULIANA   I'll come over every day to see you both.
GEORGE   Wonderful. Nobody would be more welcome.

JULIANA goes off. GEORGE goes with her. We hear him thanking her for the slippers and sending his love to Rena. HEDDA paces the room in scarcely controlled fury, her arms raised above her head, her fists clenched. She flings back the curtains on the French window and stares out. GEORGE returns.

What a sophisticated woman that is. (*He picks up the slippers*) What are you looking at?
HEDDA   The leaves. Yellow and withered already.
GEORGE   We *are* into September, you know.
HEDDA   I know — I know — don't I know.
GEORGE   Did you notice anything a little . . . different about Auntie Juju? A bit — I don't know — withdrawn?
HEDDA   I couldn't tell. I don't know her well enough.
GEORGE   I hope I didn't say anything wrong.
HEDDA   Maybe that episode with the hat offended her. I should make it up with her.
GEORGE   Ah, Hedda, would you?
HEDDA   When you see them this afternoon invite her to come over and spend the evening with us.
GEORGE   She'd like that, I know. Thank you. And there's another thing I know she'd really love: could you call her Auntie Juju?
HEDDA   That's a ridiculous name.
GEORGE   Is it? I'm so used to —
HEDDA   And we've discussed this before.
GEORGE   And you're one of the family now. Aunt Juliana?
HEDDA   You shouldn't ask this of me, George.
GEORGE   Just Juliana?

HEDDA   I will not be coerced.

GEORGE For my sake, Hedda?

HEDDA   Alright — alright — alright — I'll call her aunt.
That's as far as I'll go.

GEORGE Very generous of you. Thank you. What's the
matter?

HEDDA   My old piano. Completely out of place with these
furnishings.

GEORGE As soon as my salary starts coming through we'll
see about selling it and maybe getting a new one.

HEDDA   No, no, I'm not going to part with it. I want to put
it in there (*back room*) and I want a new one in here.

GEORGE I suppose we could look into it.

>   *She picks up a bunch of flowers from the top of the
>   piano.*

HEDDA   These weren't here when we got in last night.

GEORGE Auntie Juju probably brought them for you.

HEDDA   (*Reads card*) 'Will come back very soon. Mrs . . . '

GEORGE Who?

HEDDA   'Elvsted. Mrs T Elvsted.'

GEORGE Thea Elvsted! Really! Thea Rysing that used to be!

HEDDA   Thea Rysing indeed. An old flame of yours — am I
right?

GEORGE For all of a week, Hedda. Long before I knew you.

HEDDA   Haven't seen her — not since we were at school
together. A 'sincere' creature, I remember; and
anxious, so anxious. With a mass of ridiculous
golden curls that she thought were her great asset
and kept flaunting them. Why is she calling on us?

GEORGE Going off her head, I suspect, in that awful back-
water she lives in — somewhere away up near
Trondheim, isn't it? I remember hearing she married an elderly resident magistrate up there.

HEDDA   Didn't he move up there, too, to the Trondheim
area, Eilert Loevborg?

GEORGE D'you know, you're right! What in God's name
brought him away up there?

BERTHA *enters.*

BERTHA She's back, Madam, the lady who brought the flowers earlier.

HEDDA Well, show her in.

> BERTHA *shows* THEA ELVSTED *in and retires.* THEA ELVSTED *is an attractive woman of slight build. A few years younger than* HEDDA. *Her hair is abundant and golden. Her blue eyes are alert. She carries with her an air of diffidence, of vague anxiety. But behind that is a woman of resolution and determination.* HEDDA *greets her warmly.*

Mrs Elvsted! Lovely to see you again.

THEA And you, Mrs Tesman. It has been a long time.

HEDDA Far too long. And thank you for the flowers. They are beautiful.

THEA You're welcome.

GEORGE (*His hand out*) Too long indeed, Mrs Elvsted. Good to see you.

THEA And very belated congratulations on your wedding. I wish you both a long and happy life together.

HEDDA Thank you.

GEORGE When did you get into town?

THEA Around lunchtime yesterday. I came straight here. And when you weren't here — I can't tell you — I felt suddenly desolate, desperate almost.

HEDDA What's the matter, Mrs Elvsted? Here, take a seat.

THEA It's so reassuring to be here with you both.

HEDDA Sit down here.

THEA I can't. I'm too —

HEDDA (*Firmly*) Sit here, Mrs Elvsted. Sit.

> *She draws her to the couch and sits beside her.*

GEORGE What is it?

HEDDA Something's happened at home — isn't that it?

GEORGE Maybe we can help.

HEDDA Something to do with your husband?

THEA No, no, not really him. Well, partly him. It's — it's — it's —

GEORGE Take your time.

THEA Eilert Loevborg is here.

HEDDA (*Softly*) Oh my God.

GEORGE Here — in town?

THEA For the past week.

GEORGE D'you hear that, Hedda? Loevborg is —

HEDDA (*Sharply*) I heard.

THEA Back in this treacherous environment that almost destroyed him a few years ago. And nobody to look after him. How can he survive? He can't. He'll go under again.

HEDDA Eilert Loevborg isn't your responsibility, Mrs Elvsted.

THEA I know that. But he was my children's tutor and I feel some responsibility for him. No, not my children — I don't have a family — my husband's children.

GEORGE And was he — forgive me — I mean I wouldn't have thought Loevborg was sufficiently in control of his life to be a tutor.

THEA He's a new man, Eilert. He has himself completely in hand now. For the past three years his behaviour has been impeccable.

GEORGE D'you hear that, Hedda? His behaviour has been —

HEDDA (*Sharply*) I heard.

THEA A complete turnaround. Eilert Loevborg is now exemplary.

HEDDA Really?

THEA But I'm frightened for him here, back in all the old haunts with all those sleezy hangers-on. And now with money in his pocket! He's bound to collapse again, isn't he?

GEORGE But why didn't he stay up in Trondheim with you and your husband?

THEA How could he? — all the excitement with the new book — strangers stopping him in the street —

reporters knocking at the door — scores of letters every day. He got so excited, so agitated. How could he be held in Trondheim? He had to get to the city.

GEORGE (*To* HEDDA) Auntie Juju mentioned something about that book.

THEA A cultural history of Europe, no less. And an instant success when it came out a fortnight ago. It's in its fifth reprint.

GEORGE So this isn't a reworking of that old monograph he published seven years ago?

THEA No, no. This is altogether new. And all done in the past eighteen months when he was living with us.

GEORGE Well, well, well. Good for Loevborg, that's what I say. Loevborg resurrectus. Excellent news, Hedda, isn't it?

HEDDA *does not respond.*

THEA Eilert Loevborg, the celebrated author!

HEDDA Have you met him here in town?

THEA I managed to find his address only this morning.

HEDDA Why didn't your husband come down to look after him? He's your husband's friend, isn't he?

THEA He's caught up at the assizes. Anyhow I had shopping to do.

HEDDA (*Smiling*) Well, of course.

THEA *rises to leave.*

THEA He'll certainly drop in to see you. You and he work in the same field, don't you?

GEORGE Adjoining fields.

THEA And he's so fond of both of you — I know that.

GEORGE And we're really fond of Eilert. Aren't we, Hedda?

HEDDA *does not respond.*

THEA Who can resist Eilert? My husband thinks the world

of him, too. If he does drop in, you'll take care of him, won't you? Without the anchor of a home he'll just drift.

GEORGE Anything we can do for Eilert Loevborg — anything in the world — we'll be happy to do it.

HEDDA Don't be stupid! Eilert Loevborg isn't going to 'drop in' on us! The man's on the rampage, for God's sake — triumphant, delirious with sudden success! He's being toasted by scores of old and new friends. Even as we sit here he's probably painting the town . . . scarlet!

THEA You don't think that he's already — ?

HEDDA Do you expect him to tear himself away from that wonderful delirium and 'drop in' on this drab anchorage? Well, do you?

THEA So you think he's already lost?

HEDDA I think — if you want to save him from himself —

THEA I must. Nobody else can. When he gets into one of those manic moods he's capable of doing himself real damage.

HEDDA Then we must get him up here this very day. George will write to him.

GEORGE Good idea, Hedda.

THEA Would you?

GEORGE Of course — of course.

THEA Here is his address.

HEDDA And the quicker the better.

GEORGE I'll write him just now.

HEDDA A formal invitation; but make it very warm. You *do* want him to come, George, don't you?

GEORGE *pauses briefly.*

GEORGE Why wouldn't I want Eilert to come?

GEORGE *goes to the door. Pauses.*

My slippers.

He takes his slippers and prepares to exit.

THEA (*Calling*) Don't say anything about me having asked you.

He puts his fingers to his lips and disappears.

I pray to God he comes, Mrs Tesman.

HEDDA Yes, he'll come. You're too anxious; get a hold of yourself. And now we've got George out of the way we can really talk. Sit down here beside me.

They sit together on the sofa. HEDDA *takes* THEA's *hand in hers.*

THEA I'll have to go very soon, Mrs Tesman.

HEDDA 'Mrs Tesman — Mrs Tesman'! I'm sick of damn convention. It's Hedda — Hedda! Weren't we at school together? You knew me as Hedda and I knew you as Thea.

THEA You were a year ahead of me.

HEDDA Yes, about that.

THEA I was terrified of you.

HEDDA Thea!

THEA When we met on the stair you used to pull my hair.

HEDDA Wasn't I a little brat!

THEA And you told me once you'd like to set fire to it.

HEDDA (*Laughs*) I never did!

THEA You meant it, too.

HEDDA Oh my God, what a demon I must have been!

THEA I really *was* terrified of you.

HEDDA Can you ever forgive me?

THEA And then you were the daughter of General Gabler and my father was a storeman on the docks. That was another chasm. Anyhow . . . a long time ago . . . I really must leave.

HEDDA No, no, you can't leave now, Thea. Wait until George writes his letter. Things haven't been going so well at home, have they?

THEA I'd rather not talk about that.

HEDDA You haven't forgiven me. Oh, Thea. (*Kisses* THEA's *cheek*) I am sorry. How can I make it up to you?

THEA What is there to make up?

HEDDA You're not accustomed to kindness, Thea, are you? Even at home?

THEA I haven't got a home. I never had a home.

HEDDA You have the Elvsted home.

THEA Just an address.

HEDDA You first went there as a housekeeper, didn't you?

THEA I was employed as a governess. But his wife — his late wife — became very ill and eventually was invalided and I had to look after all the household affairs as well.

HEDDA And you ended up mistress of the house?

THEA Yes.

HEDDA And then you and Mr Elvsted got married?

THEA Five years ago.

HEDDA And wasn't Eilert Loevborg up there the last three years?

THEA Yes.

HEDDA Had you known him before that?

THEA Not really. I knew *of* him of course.

HEDDA So he stayed in the Elvsted house?

THEA I couldn't do the teaching and manage the household.

HEDDA So he took on the tutoring job?

THEA Yes.

HEDDA And I suppose your husband has to be away a lot?

THEA He has a huge area to cover; a great deal of travelling.

HEDDA So much was left to you then: the usual anxieties of the bourgeoisie — the children's studies — and their grinds — and the household routine — and the difficulty of getting staff. And your husband — is he a considerate man? Is he a good provider? Is he faithful?

THEA Oh yes, yes.

HEDDA Is he kind to you?

THEA He probably thinks he is.

HEDDA He's a lot older than you, isn't he?

THEA More than twenty years. We have nothing at all in common.

HEDDA Does he love you?

THEA Does he? Maybe. In his own way. I'm useful. I'm cheap. I don't know if he cares about anybody. His children, perhaps.

HEDDA He cares about Eilert Loevborg, Thea.

THEA What do you mean?

HEDDA As you say, 'Who can resist Eilert?' And he did send you down to look after him.

THEA Not at all. He was away at assizes somewhere. He doesn't even know I'm here. I just couldn't stay up there alone, Hedda. So I threw some things in a bag and walked out. I think I was hysterical.

HEDDA Not a word to anyone?

THEA I ran all the way to the station. I think I was demented.

HEDDA That was a very courageous thing to do, Thea.

THEA I don't think I had a choice.

HEDDA But what will your husband say when you go back?

THEA I'm never going back there again.

HEDDA You've left your husband, your home — your anchor — for good? And in broad daylight?

THEA Yes.

HEDDA So *you're* drifting now, Thea?

THEA Yes.

HEDDA And you don't care about a scandal, what people will say about you?

THEA Not really. Not at all, I think.

HEDDA How I envy you that courage. I wish to God I could summon that daring.

THEA Not courage, is it? I don't think I had a choice.

HEDDA Oh yes, I envy you, Thea Elvsted.

She kisses THEA *again on the cheek. Pause.*

(*Very brisk*) And now I want to know all about you and Eilert Loevborg — step by step — Thea and Eilert — every detail.

THEA Thea and Eilert . . . I tell myself it has a special euphony.

HEDDA And it has. Now. Step by step.

THEA Thea and Eilert . . . yes . . .

I used to watch him through a crack in the parlour door; teaching the children at the big, mahogany table. The stooped shoulders. The patient hands. The lank hair. But especially the face; and the cornflower-blue eyes, those hesitant, irresolute eyes that hinted at weakness. And always, always that wan, apologetic smile that confirmed that weakness. Flinching before the sly bullying of the children and my husband's crude discourtesies. I could see how damaged he was and how incapable of protecting himself: that every lesson with the children and every encounter with my husband was an occasion for humiliation. And watching him through a crack in the parlour door I suddenly knew that I loved that weak, talented, damaged Eilert Loevborg . . . yes. Loved him suddenly and fiercely and altogether without caution. A love so fierce and so palpable that I knew it could shelter him from some of those humiliations and retrieve that loss of confidence and indeed fortify him against the pull of those old excesses, just because it was so fierce a love, because it was so palpable. And that's what I did. I loved him away from his dissipations. I loved him into an accord with himself again. I even loved him into reciprocating my love for him.

And so step by step he became more resolute. And step by step the apologetic smile disappeared and he began to laugh again. And with his new self-belief he began to educate me; opened me up just by talking to me and encouraging me to respond to him; taught me to look for different choices and fresh possibilities. And so we rescued one another. I really believed that. I know I felt I had been delivered. I think he felt redeemed too. Eilert Loevborg . . . yes . . .

And then one day he asked me — out of the blue — he asked me would I help him with the new book he was planning to write, to write it *with* him. And I shocked myself — 'Of course I will,' I said. Me! The housekeeper, the daughter of the storeman on the docks! And that's what we did, Hedda: we wrote that book together; six hours a day for eighteen months. 'Collaborators' — that was his name for us. And during that eighteen months I discovered that our deliverance was more than just a liberation. It had within it an approval, maybe even a benediction on what we were doing together: Thea and Eilert, collaborators . . . And that's it, Hedda: step by step. No, I have left out a step. There is a dancer-singer-performer back in town. A creature with blazing red hair. A hussy. Eilert and she were friends once — well, acquaintances. He hasn't seen her in years. She wrote to him last week. The letter, I know, upset him. Apparently she carries a pistol in her handbag. And when they parted years ago she threatened to shoot him.

HEDDA People don't do that sort of thing.

GEORGE *approaches.*

(*Whispers*) Strictly between you and me.
THEA Oh yes, Hedda, please, please.
HEDDA Not a word.
GEORGE Here we are. Formal but *very* warm.
HEDDA Mrs Elvsted is about to leave, George. I'll walk her to the garden gate.
GEORGE Would you ask Bertha to see to this (*letter*)?
HEDDA (*Takes envelope*) I'll tell her.

BERTHA *enters.*

33

HEDDA   Drop this in the post, Berna.

BERTHA   Judge Brack is here to see you both.

HEDDA   Show him in. And post that letter immediately.

BERTHA   Yes, madam.

> BERTHA *shows* BRACK *in and then exits.* BRACK *is in his mid-forties. Elegantly dressed; a little vain; a little pompous. He is fastidious — almost precious — in his manner and speech. He is very aware that he presents this image of himself and there is a salutary undertone of self-mockery in the presentation. He prides himself in his knowledge of this new slang and these American neologisms. At the same time he uses this vocabulary with a hint of derision. He appears to be very relaxed but the mind is razor-sharp and the alert eyes miss nothing.*

BRACK   I know — I know — an unconscionable hour to call on people of feeling. Assure me I *am* welcome.

HEDDA   Always, Judge Brack.

> *He kisses her hand with — almost — mock formality.*

BRACK   The most elegant Mrs Tesman.

HEDDA   And this is Mrs Elvsted. Judge Brack.

BRACK   (*Bows*) Enchanté.

THEA   (*Ill at ease*) If you'll excuse me, Hedda —

HEDDA   You look different by daylight, Your Honour.

BRACK   Really? Should that disquiet me?

HEDDA   You look even younger.

BRACK   Mrs Tesman is elegant *and* artful.

GEORGE   And how do you think she (*Hedda*) looks, Judge? Did you notice she has put on a little —

BRACK   Much too early in the day to take cognisance of mere appearances.

HEDDA   Have you thanked the judge for all the trouble he went to for us?

GEORGE   I was about to.

BRACK   Nothing — nothing. My pleasure.

HEDDA   What we would have done without you I just don't
        know.

THEA   Sorry for fussing but I'm afraid I have to go.

BRACK   I'm interrupting something, am I?

THEA   No, no, don't think that — nothing at all — please
        don't think that. Hedda will tell you I was about
        to —

HEDDA   Yes, she's anxious to get away.

THEA   (*To* BRACK) Very pleased to meet you. I hope we
        meet again very . . . soon.

BRACK   As do I.

THEA   Goodbye, George.

GEORGE The flowers are lovely.

THEA   Congratulations again.

        THEA *and* HEDDA *exit.*

BRACK   You've had a look around. Is your lady wife happy
        with it all?

GEORGE Thank you *so* much. Everything's just perfect.

BRACK   Splendid.

GEORGE We'll probably move things round a bit.

BRACK   Of course.

GEORGE And she tells me she still has a few more items she
        has to buy.

BRACK   (*Concerned*) Items?

GEORGE God knows what. Nothing for you to be concerned
        about. Have a seat.

BRACK   There is something I think we should talk about,
        George.

GEORGE Money.

BRACK   Good Lord, no! We can anguish over that later.
        Though I do wish the furnishings were a little more
        . . . demure.

GEORGE Impossible, Judge. You know Hedda — anything
        more modest and she would just wilt.

BRACK   (*Wryly*) Really?

GEORGE And when the professorship comes through we'll
        be comfortably on top of our finances again.

BRACK These matters take time, Tesman.

GEORGE Have you heard something?

BRACK Nothing reliable . . . rumours . . . gossip. Yes, I did hear one bit of interesting tattle: your old friend, Eilert Loevborg, is back in town.

GEORGE So Mrs Elvsted told me.

BRACK Mrs — ?

GEORGE Elvsted. The magistrate's wife. You've just met her.

BRACK Of course. A lady addicted to her anxieties, I suspect.

GEORGE (*Laughs*) Is she? Anyhow, Loevborg has been living with the Elvsteds in the outskirts of Trondheim.

BRACK And turned over a new leaf, would you believe.

GEORGE He has!

BRACK A completely reformed character, they say.

GEORGE Yes!

BRACK Like our friend, Saint Paul. But I'm afraid my dubious trade has taught me to be wary of sudden conversions.

GEORGE And he has a new book out. Everybody's talking about it.

BRACK So I hear.

GEORGE A huge popular success, apparently.

BRACK I'll be candid with you, George: I never did believe in Paul's conversion. I mean, tumbling off a horse and all that circus stuff . . . Quite improbable.

GEORGE (*Laughs*) Judge!

BRACK Loevborg's new book? Oh yes, an enormous success. 'Jumbo', as I'm told the Americans have it. Jumbo — rather sweet, isn't it?

GEORGE He's such a gifted man. And only a few years ago everyone had written him off. He should make some money on this. But the question is: when this fuss dies down, what will he live on?

HEDDA *enters.*

HEDDA George's persistent worry about everybody: 'What will he live on?' What will who live on?

GEORGE Poor old Loevborg. The money his uncle left him a few years ago, that must be long gone. And he can't produce a new book every year. So what will become of him?

HEDDA Or any of us.

GEORGE Sorry?

BRACK He has relatives in the town who still have a lot of clout. (*To himself*) 'Clout'? — sounds like an Americanism, too, doesn't it?

GEORGE They've washed their hands of him.

BRACK Their golden boy?

GEORGE Haven't spoken to him in years.

BRACK Say what you like, he *has* produced a successful book.

HEDDA So then Elvsted was right: she *has* delivered him.

   Pause.

BRACK (*Pretended confusion*) Where to?

HEDDA (*Laughs*) Rescued him, Judge! — redeemed him! Loevborg is *saved*.

   BRACK *crosses his arms before his face to ward off evil.*

BRACK Saved?! Oh good God! That word terrifies me! I will not have it!

HEDDA You shouldn't worry. It's not something you're likely to experience.

GEORGE Well, maybe they'll find something for him. He is such a brilliant man. By the way, Hedda, I've asked him over to dinner this evening.

BRACK But you're coming to my bachelor party this evening. I invited you down at the quay last night.

HEDDA Had you forgotten, George?

GEORGE Sorry — I'm afraid I did — my apologies — I really am sorry, Judge.

BRACK Don't worry. Loevborg won't turn up here.

HEDDA Why won't he?

BRACK gets to his feet.

BRACK   There's something both of you ought to know.

GEORGE   About Eilert?

BRACK   About Eilert. About you, too. The professorship — the actual appointment — may not come through as easily or as quickly as we hoped. In fact I'm told they've decided to advertise the post again. So the job may well attract many new applicants.

HEDDA   Like Loevborg?

BRACK   Indeed.

GEORGE   Oh my goodness, do you hear that, Hedda?

HEDDA   (*Softly. Immobile*) Interesting.

GEORGE   But this is outrageous! For God's sake I was practically promised that job! I've just got married! I got married on the strength of that job! We've got huge debts! And we've borrowed money from Auntie Juju!

BRACK   And I expect you'll get it. You'll just have to take part in a competition.

HEDDA   (*Softly. Immobile*) It will be a kind of duel, won't it?

GEORGE   How can you be so damned calm, Hedda?

HEDDA   I can hardly wait for the outcome.

BRACK   Anyhow, it's just as well you know how things stand, Mrs Tesman — before you decide on buying any extra items.

HEDDA   My plans won't change, Judge.

BRACK   Probably not. Knowing you. And now I must leave you. (*To* GEORGE) I'll pick you up this evening on my way home from my walk.

GEORGE   (*Confused*) Yes — please — yes — do that if you would — forgive me, I'm a little . . .

HEDDA   Goodbye, Judge. I'll see you later.

BRACK   Au revoir. I'm wrong — it's not an Americanism, 'clout'. An archery term — the mark shot at — a fair clout. Glad I got that. Until this evening.

He exits.

GEORGE He's making all that up, isn't he?

HEDDA (*Innocently*) The mark shot at?

GEORGE About a competition. Just to keep me on my toes, isn't it? Dear God, I'm shattered, Hedda. Look — I'm shaking. He's right: the job's gone, isn't it? It is, isn't it? Yes, it's gone. Was it all a fantasy? It just shows, you can't live out your daydreams, doesn't it?

HEDDA Is that what you're doing?

GEORGE I don't know. Is it? Got married; bought our dream house; furnished it stylishly — all on an expectation. It wasn't all a daydream, Hedda, was it?

HEDDA We agreed to live in a certain style.

GEORGE We did, didn't we? And I wanted all that so much, really for you, only for you: a splendid house, a circle of close friends, and at the heart of it all, my Hedda, my beautiful, translucent Hedda. I'm sorry, my love. This isn't what you deserve.

HEDDA So no butler?

GEORGE (*Bleak laugh*) No butler.

HEDDA And the bay mare you promised me?

GEORGE Oh God no, Hedda. Sorry. The cost and upkeep —

HEDDA Well, I have at least one thing to amuse me.

GEORGE What's that?

HEDDA My father's pistols.

GEORGE (*Alarmed*) Pistols?

HEDDA The pistols General Gabler left me.

As she exits:

GEORGE (*Calling*) For heaven's sake, Hedda, don't even touch those awful things. Please, love. For my sake, darling . . . Oh my goodness . . .

End of Act One. Quick black.

ACT TWO

Tesmans' drawing room, early afternoon of the same day. The piano is gone and in its place an elegant writing table and a bookcase. Most of the flowers have been removed. Mrs Elvsted's bouquet now sits in the centre of the table.

HEDDA is alone on stage, standing beside the open French windows. She is loading a pistol. There is an identical pistol in the open pistol-case on the table. HEDDA is wearing a beautiful dress.

HEDDA (*Looking out*) Judge Brack, if you don't mind!

BRACK (*Off*) It is indeed, Mrs Tesman.

HEDDA Back again, Your Honour.

BRACK (*Off*) A man of my word.

She raises the pistol and takes aim.

HEDDA You're right in my sights, Judge Brack.

BRACK (*Off*) Sorry?

HEDDA I'm about to take a shot at you.

BRACK (*Off*) Don't point that thing at me!

HEDDA This will teach you not to slip in the back way.

She fires.

BRACK Jesus Christ, woman! Are you out of your mind?

HEDDA I think I missed.

BRACK (*Off*) Stop that at once, Hedda! D'you hear me? At once!

HEDDA Aren't you coming in?

He enters through the French windows. He is very angry. He is wearing a dress suit for his bachelor party. Hat. Coat. Gloves.

40

HEDDA Your Honour's looking very dashing this evening.
BRACK What do you think you're doing, woman? What in God's name are you shooting at?
HEDDA You. The great blue sky. Whatever. It's only a game, Judge.

He takes the gun from her hand.

BRACK If you don't mind, Mrs Tesman. That's criminal behaviour. Where's the case?

He puts the gun away.

HEDDA Just passing the time. You can be such a churl.
BRACK Enough of that little game for today. Where's George?
HEDDA The moment he finished lunch, off he scampered to the aunties. You're early, aren't you?
BRACK Had I known he wasn't here I would have come even earlier.
HEDDA And there would have been no one to receive you.
BRACK Just you alone.
HEDDA I have been up in my bedroom all afternoon, dressing.
BRACK Couldn't I at least have . . . considered you through a crack in your bedroom door?
HEDDA There is no crack in the bedroom door, Judge.
BRACK You'll have to rectify that, won't you?
HEDDA George won't be home for some time. You'll have to be patient.
BRACK I'm a man of almost saintly patience. Let's have a talk, you and I.
HEDDA We haven't had a real talk for ages.
BRACK You mean *à deux*?
HEDDA I believe I do.
BRACK You were away so long, Hedda, I was beginning to despair of ever seeing you again.
HEDDA I thought myself I'd never get back.
BRACK From your exciting honeymoon?

HEDDA (*Ironically*) Thrilling.

BRACK George found it exciting — according to his letters.

HEDDA Burrowing into archives, grubbing around old libraries, copying out old documents faithfully, faithfully — that's the only thing that excites George.

BRACK That *is* his profession.

HEDDA I can't tell you how bored I was.

BRACK Come on!

HEDDA I know it sounds abnormal but my honeymoon bored me. Am I unnatural?

BRACK (*Laughs*) You?!

HEDDA Bored — bored — bored.

BRACK I'm secretly delighted of course. But you just can't have been bored for the entire six months?

HEDDA Have you any idea what it's like not to meet even one other person you could have a conversation with during that entire time?

BRACK None.

HEDDA Or the purgatory of spending the twenty-four hours of every single day with the same person?

BRACK Hell. (*Quickly*) Forgive me — forgive me. George Tesman is an upright and thoroughly decent man — and a worthy academic, I'm sure. I have considerable respect for George Tesman.

HEDDA 'Considerable — ' You know, you practise your little cruelties very skilfully.

BRACK Goes with the job. But, Hedda, you married the man so you must have loved him.

HEDDA That's sentimental.

BRACK You *did* marry him.

HEDDA Who could resist domestic crafts in tenth-century Holland and cottage industries in east Belgium? For God's sake, man! Yes, I did marry him — is that altogether bizarre?

BRACK Yes, there was a time when it did look as if George was going to be a great academic star. We all believed that.

HEDDA That's not why I married him. That didn't interest

me. I married him because I had danced myself to a standstill. Because — may I be melodramatic, Judge? — because I had an instinct things had come to an end for me, that it was all played out. So in panic, despair maybe, I latched on to what was stable and dependable.

BRACK Stable and dependable George Tesman.

HEDDA By God he is.

BRACK And quite a decent scholar, I'm assured. Don't overlook that.

HEDDA And not at all ridiculous?

BRACK What a strange word to use, Hedda. No, no, I wouldn't say ridiculous.

HEDDA An anchor then?

BRACK Oh yes, an anchor.

HEDDA And since he genuinely wanted to take care of me, why wouldn't I allow him? That's not what my other men friends had in mind.

BRACK I'm sure we all cared deeply for you, Hedda.

HEDDA Caring for me was never uppermost in your mind, Judge.

BRACK Constantly. And I ask nothing more from life than a small group of people I can trust and hold dear and can help when help is needed and into whose houses I can come and go as freely as I wish — as a friend.

HEDDA Of the husband?

BRACK The wife preferably. But don't misunderstand me: my respect for the institution of marriage borders on the sacred.

HEDDA Judge!

BRACK In theory.

HEDDA You're a scamp, Judge Brack.

BRACK Me?

HEDDA A rogue.

BRACK Am I?

HEDDA A smooth scoundrel.

BRACK Never.

HEDDA And maybe even malevolent at heart.

BRACK   Humiliate me. Enjoy your little jape. Alright, I will confess to one small vice — no, no, vice is a judgemental word; a little weakness, a minor delinquency; indeed some people find it a fetching weakness.

HEDDA   Confess.

BRACK   I must have the companionship and the consolations of women very regularly. It's a most pressing exigency. It's the only passion of my youth that has stayed faithful to me, thank heaven. Yes, I do believe that this domestic triangle arrangement can be enriching for everybody. Answer me truthfully: when you were on those interminable train journeys in Austria — those dreary forests, that dreary food, those dreary people, those execrable peasant costumes they *will* exhibit themselves in — wouldn't you have bartered something you really cherished for a little naughty prattle — soupçon of salacious gossip?

HEDDA   I would have bartered everything.

BRACK   Well, dear Mrs Tesman, the honeymoon's over.

HEDDA   It's not, you know. The train has only stopped at a station.

BRACK   So jump off and stretch your legs.

HEDDA   I'm not the jumping sort.

BRACK   In the dark vault of their hearts all women are jumpers.

HEDDA   Far too cautious to jump. There's always somebody spying on you, carrying stories back. So I'll stay in the compartment — just chatting — *à deux.*

BRACK   Not at all safe and altogether miserable.

HEDDA   Too frightened to jump; terrified of scandal.

BRACK   And suppose a friend were to join you in the compartment? A trusted friend, one of a small group?

HEDDA   That's very different.

BRACK   A desperately weak man?

HEDDA   But a fetching weakness.

BRACK   Totally unsafe and exceedingly naughty?

HEDDA   Yes, that would be different.

BRACK   That would interest you?

HEDDA   No jumping expected?

BRACK   No jumping, no melodrama, and certainly no pistols.

HEDDA   That could well be attractive, Judge Brack.

The sound of the door opening.

BRACK   (*Softly*) I do believe the triangle is complete, Miss Hedda. And completion is a satisfaction in itself, isn't it?

HEDDA   (*Softly*) And the train moves on.

GEORGE *enters, perspiring, laden with books and academic journals.*

GEORGE   It's very hot out there, Hedda. And these things weigh a ton. (*Sees* BRACK) Judge, you're here! Why didn't Bertha tell me?

BRACK   Came in the back way.

GEORGE   I'm not late, am I?

BRACK   I'm early.

GEORGE   I have time for a wash then. I'm sweating, lugging these all over town.

HEDDA   What have you got?

GEORGE   New publications that appeared while our backs were turned. Sneaked out, you could say. And a heap of academic journals and monographs and lectures and essays.

BRACK   All to do with your special subject?

GEORGE   Be away for even a short time and they seem to plot behind your back.

HEDDA   You must have a surfeit of that stuff.

GEORGE   All vital if you want to stay on top. And look, Hedda, Loevborg's new book. Dipped into it in the bookshop. Would you like to look at it?

HEDDA   Not now. Later. Maybe.

BRACK   And what's your verdict, Tesman, as an expert yourself?

GEORGE   A remarkable accomplishment, balanced, well organized, persuasively argued. But what's really interesting is that it's written in a light and clean style that's altogether new for Loevborg.

BRACK   Gee whiz — as the Americans have it.

GEORGE   Full of surprises is our Eilert, isn't he?

BRACK   (*To* HEDDA) Light and clean — part of his deliverance, perhaps?

GEORGE   He is an astonishing creature. I'll go and freshen up. (*To* BRACK) We don't have to dash off just now?

BRACK   No hurry.

GEORGE   (*To* HEDDA) By the way Auntie Juju won't be coming over this evening.

HEDDA   Still sulking about that hat business?

GEORGE   Oh no. How could you think that of her, Hedda? No, it's Auntie Rena. She's still very ill.

HEDDA   She usually is.

GEORGE   Yes, but this looks like a serious turn.

HEDDA   Then of course the other one must stay with her. I'll just have to make do without her, won't I?

GEORGE   She sends you her love. And she was so pleased to see how nicely you've filled out.

HEDDA   (*Icily*) Was she?

GEORGE   (*Coyly, to* BRACK) She keeps studying Hedda for — you know — tell-tale symptoms. All very innocent and that little bit daring.

HEDDA   (*Softly*) Interfering bitch.

GEORGE *exits.*

BRACK   Temper, Miss Hedda. What's this hat business?

HEDDA   'Auntie Juju' left her hat on the chair this morning. (*Smiling*) I pretended I thought it was the maid's.

BRACK   So you practise your own little cruelties?

HEDDA   Yes. And more frequently. And with more relish. Should that worry me, Judge?

BRACK   A pinch of malevolence gives life an interesting tang.

HEDDA   Every so often a dark impulse takes hold of me.

I feel I've actually been invaded and taken over — (*Smiles*) it's called possession in the Bible, isn't it?

BRACK (*Shrugs*) Wouldn't know.

HEDDA Sometimes it's just a capricious force — poor Auntie Juju got only a tiny scratch. But it's becoming bitter and cruel. While it possesses me I'm not responsible for anything I say or do. A sort of joyless freedom. Afterwards of course I loathe myself. A little frightening, isn't it?

BRACK I find most women can be a little . . . capricious.

HEDDA You're playing with me, Judge.

BRACK Sorry.

HEDDA When it controls me I find I even seek out my quarry. And the most vulnerable prey and the one I'm most fearful of hurting — you probably won't believe this — I'm most fearful of damaging George.

BRACK George, the anchor. Decent George Tesman. I wouldn't be concerned for George, Hedda. That kind of simple decency has an immunity of its own. But what can I say to you? It's probably a passing mood. Marriage can be traumatic, especially for a woman of such fiercely independent spirit. Try to focus on all the good things — all the happy things around you.

HEDDA (*Sharply*) What are all the good and happy things around me?

BRACK You have a beautiful home, the house you set your heart on.

HEDDA That damned fiction has hardened into fact.

BRACK You didn't want this house?

HEDDA What happened was this. All last summer George used to walk me home from dances and —

BRACK My house lay in the opposite direction; pity.

HEDDA Your interests lay in another direction, too, Judge.

BRACK Saucy. Anyhow — ?

HEDDA Anyhow we were passing this house one night and George had run out of something to talk about — literally he had nothing more to say — he couldn't

speak. So to help him out of his misery I pointed
up to this place and off the top of my head I said
there was nowhere else in the whole world I'd
rather live than here. One of those capricious im-
pulses.

BRACK   And that was it?

HEDDA   The fantasy was born.

BRACK   So you don't give a curse about this place?

HEDDA   Not a single curse. It reeks of lavender and dried
flowers — like a funeral parlour.

BRACK   And after all the work we did to bedizen it for you.
Part of your trouble, young lady, is that you have
nothing to think about except yourself. What you
must do is take up something that would engage
you fully. Have you any interest in painting?

HEDDA   (*Savagely*) The judge means a hobby! Oh clever
Judge Brack! No, painting doesn't interest me. But
what about that old Turkish craft of macramé? Or
bee-keeping perhaps? Or collecting miniature lead
soldiers? Surely that would have a special interest
for a general's daughter?

BRACK   Of course we're going to be bored if we keep
brooding on our little restricted lives. Look outside
yourself and beyond these confines and —

HEDDA   He's so wise. We're liable to implode just because
we don't see that perfect little petunia out there, or
the chaste moon peeping out from behind that
cloud, or the smile on baby's face when it hears its
darling mummy.

BRACK   Isn't it possible — indeed very probable — that a
certain happy event will alter the whole tenor of
your life here?

HEDDA   That silly stuff about the professorship? Doesn't
interest me in the —

BRACK   I mean you may suddenly find yourself — as most
young brides do — being handed the wonderful
and exciting responsibility —

HEDDA   Judge Brack has joined the coy brigade! 'Isn't
she filling out interestingly?' Good God, the man's

actually smirking!

BRACK But it *is* more than likely.

HEDDA Never! D'you hear me? Never! Give me miniature soldiers any day — leaden soldiers! Ah, the professor.

> GEORGE *enters. He is dressed formally for Brack's party.*

GEORGE No sign of Loevborg yet?

HEDDA No.

GEORGE He should be here soon.

BRACK If he's coming.

GEORGE Oh yes, he'll come. (*To* BRACK) And what you said about him this morning is just gossip. Auntie Juju says he wouldn't dare block my promotion again.

BRACK Then everything is . . . hunky-dory?

GEORGE When does your party begin, Judge?

BRACK Nobody will turn up until seven — seven-thirty. We're in no hurry.

HEDDA You don't have to wait around here on my account. I'll have Loevborg and Mrs Elvsted.

BRACK (*To* GEORGE. *Softly*) Mrs — ?

GEORGE (*Softly back*) Addicted-to-her-anxieties Thea.

BRACK Ah.

HEDDA We'll chatter and laugh and drink strong Darjeeling tea.

BRACK Tea is sensible. Mr Loevborg might be advised to avoid my domicile.

HEDDA Why?

BRACK Haven't you always averred that only men of iron discipline and heroic virtue should be allowed into my parties?

HEDDA Then Eilert Loevborg qualifies on both counts.

BRACK Has he — ?

HEDDA I told you, Judge — *saved.*

> BRACK *crosses his arms before his face — to ward off evil.*

BRACK (*Pretended terror*) Good God yes, you did!

BERTHA *enters.*

BERTHA There's a gentleman here to see you, Mrs Tesman.
GEORGE Loevborg! You see!
HEDDA (*To* BERTHA) Show him in.
BRACK Does he have a halo?
HEDDA Careful.
BRACK Haloes make me queasy.
HEDDA Careful.
GEORGE I knew he'd come. All gossip, Judge.

EILERT LOEVBORG *enters. He is about the same age
as* TESMAN *but looks older and is slightly haggard.
He speaks softly. He seems ill at ease.*

GEORGE Eilert! After all these years! Welcome!
LOEVBORG Thank you for your warm letter. (*Hand out*) Mrs
Tesman.
HEDDA Yes, you're most welcome.
LOEVBORG I haven't seen you since your big day. Congratula-
tions to you both.
HEDDA Thank you. You know Judge Brack?
LOEVBORG We've met.
BRACK It has been some time.
GEORGE And you're moving back into town again?
Excellent! You must come and go in this house as
freely as you wish. Mustn't he, Hedda?
HEDDA He'll have his own place.
GEORGE And I got your new book this afternoon. Well
done! Can't wait to get stuck into it.
LOEVBORG Don't bother. It's not serious.
GEORGE Come on, Eilert!
LOEVBORG I mean that. Pot-boiler stuff.
BRACK It's a big success, as you know.
LOEVBORG That's what I set out to write: a welcoming book,
no demands whatever.
BRACK You certainly succeeded, a huge success. I'm all for

... jumbo.

LOEVBORG I wanted to get my name back up there again.

BRACK Don't we all want to be embraced? (*To* HEDDA) And nobody more than lonely judges.

GEORGE Don't listen to that. I've dipped into it and I got a whiff of something very engaging.

LOEVBORG Bogus all the same.

HEDDA Don't be so stern with yourself. The public isn't nearly as austere as you.

LOEVBORG But I *do* know, Mrs Tesman. (*He produces a large envelope*) Now this is the real thing.

GEORGE (*Shocked*) Not another new book?

LOEVBORG Yes. The authentic thing. The genuine article. This is my important book. (*Suddenly embarrassed*) At least it's not as easy to see through this one.

BRACK Congratulations, Sir.

GEORGE Congratulations indeed, Eilert.

BRACK What a fecund young man! Two books back to back! As we say . . . jeepers creepers!

GEORGE What is this one about?

LOEVBORG It's a sequel.

GEORGE To what?

LOEVBORG The last one — the one that's just out.

GEORGE But the one that's just out — doesn't that take us right up to the present?

LOEVBORG This one goes beyond that.

GEORGE What do you mean, Eilert?

LOEVBORG This one reaches into the future.

GEORGE So it's speculative — a kind of divination?

LOEVBORG Not really. It's made up of two parts. The first part analyses the role and the power of the arts in our society today.

GEORGE (*Leafing through the manuscript*) This isn't your writing, is it?

LOEVBORG I dictated it. And the second part, the core of the book, looks at the way this society will develop under these artistic pressures.

GEORGE (*Barely concealed dejection*) Astonishing, Eilert! Well done. I could never tackle anything on that scale.

LOEVBORG I thought I might read a few pages to you this evening . . . just to give you a taste . . . perhaps?

GEORGE That would be great. But this evening, I'm afraid —

LOEVBORG Of course — of course — some other time —

BRACK We're having a small dinner party at my place this evening —

LOEVBORG Doesn't matter —

BRACK — to celebrate the groom's return.

LOEVBORG Lovely.

BRACK Would you like to join us?

LOEVBORG (*Firmly*) No, I can't do that. Thank you.

BRACK Just a gathering of friends anticipating a few simple pleasures, and not, as Mrs Tesman insists, hell-bent on debauchery.

LOEVBORG Maybe another time.

BRACK You could read your manuscript to Tesman at my place.

GEORGE Good idea.

BRACK Big house; plenty room.

GEORGE Yes! What do you say, Eilert?

HEDDA Mr Loevborg doesn't want to go, George. He'll stay here and have a simple supper with me and Mrs Elvsted. (*To* LOEVBORG) Is that alright?

LOEVBORG I'd love to. Thank you. Mrs Elvsted is coming here? I ran into her this afternoon.

HEDDA Yes. The three of us will have a miniature debauch here.

HEDDA *rings for* BERTHA. *When* BERTHA *enters* HEDDA *whispers instructions to her.* BERTHA *exits. Meanwhile:*

GEORGE And they tell me in the bookshop you're going to do a series of readings from your new book.

LOEVBORG In the autumn. That's the plan.

GEORGE That'll be a very successful tour.

BRACK Excerpts from . . . jumbo?

GEORGE (*Puzzled*) Sorry?

LOEVBORG You don't mind, do you?

GEORGE No, no, no. Why should I mind?

LOEVBORG I won't cut across your plans in any way?

GEORGE I can't expect you to cancel everything just because —

LOEVBORG If you like I can wait until after you've been appointed professor.

GEORGE But we're competing against one another, aren't we?

LOEVBORG No, no, you take the professorship.

GEORGE Me?

LOEVBORG Why not? I've no interest in it now.

GEORGE Eilert, you're not serious?

LOEVBORG Very serious. I'll be happy with a *succès d'estime*.

GEORGE You mean you're not — ?

LOEVBORG I've withdrawn my name.

GEORGE (*Softly*) Gaudeamus! Auntie Juju was right, Hedda! Eilert isn't going to stand in our way!

HEDDA *Our* way? Nothing to do with me, has it?

> HEDDA *goes to the back room where* BERTHA *is putting glasses and a jug on the table.* HEDDA *returns to the drawing room.* GEORGE *continues:*

GEORGE (*Shocked*) There you are, Judge! Withdrawn — you see?

BRACK So yet another honour is about to descend on you.

GEORGE I'm struck dumb!

BRACK Congratulations. Of course you're pleased.

GEORGE I am — I am — I am — I am! Thank you so much! Very kind of you, Judge! You're much, much too generous.

HEDDA Are you alright?

GEORGE I'm stunned! Flabbergasted! Oh my goodness . . .

BRACK In our small group, Hedda, a success for one is a success for all.

HEDDA (*Quickly*) I've cold punch in there. Who's for a glass?

BRACK Splendid. Professor?

GEORGE Yes! By God, yes, indeed yes!

53

HEDDA	Mr Loevborg?
LOEVBORG	Not for me, thank you.
BRACK	Only cold punch, man. It's not poison.
LOEVBORG	Not for you maybe.
HEDDA	You two go inside. I'll entertain Mr Loevborg here.
GEORGE	Do that, Hedda. Eilert Loevborg is a major artist and a very, very great man.

BRACK and GEORGE go into the back room where they drink and chat and smoke. HEDDA picks up a photograph album from the writing desk.

HEDDA	Could you endure this? — holiday photographs. I know — guaranteed to bore.
LOEVBORG	I'd love to see them.
HEDDA	Worse — honeymoon photographs — the ultimate boredom.

She sits in a corner of the couch. He stands looking down at her. Then he takes a chair beside her, his back to the other room. HEDDA is a little uneasy and speaks more loudly than necessary.

	Mostly of the Tyrol. You've never been there? Exciting forests, exciting food, exciting people; and their magnificent peasant costumes. And these are the Ortler mountains. See? — George has written the name so carefully underneath: 'O-r-t-l- '
LOEVBORG	Hedda — Gabler.
HEDDA	Shhh.
LOEVBORG	Hedda — Gabler.
HEDDA	That used to be my name. Not now.
LOEVBORG	Can I never say Hedda Gabler again?
HEDDA	I'm not Hedda Gabler any longer.
LOEVBORG	Yes, you're Hedda Tesman now. For God's sake, how could you?
HEDDA	Stop it at once!

GEORGE approaches.

And this is the Ampezzo valley. And those mountains — they're a bit hazy — they're — what's the name of that range, George?

GEORGE Let me see.

HEDDA You're slipping. No careful name written at the bottom.

GEORGE The Dolomites.

HEDDA Of course — the Dolomites.

GEORGE A glass of punch, Hedda?

HEDDA Please. And some canapés.

GEORGE A cigarette?

HEDDA Not just now.

GEORGE Certainly, madam.

> GEORGE *returns to* BRACK. *Every so often* BRACK
> *looks sharply at* HEDDA *and* LOEVBORG.

LOEVBORG For God's sake how could you, Hedda?

HEDDA And that's the Dolomites again from the other side of the valley.

LOEVBORG Answer me, Hedda.

HEDDA If you keep calling me Hedda I won't talk to you at all.

LOEVBORG Not even when we're alone?

HEDDA Think it if you want but don't say it.

LOEVBORG Because you love George Tesman?

HEDDA Now you're being ridiculous.

LOEVBORG Don't you love him?

HEDDA I will not be unfaithful. Is that understood?

LOEVBORG Then tell me this, Hedda: why did you — ?

HEDDA Shhh.

> GEORGE *returns with a tray, glasses, canapés.*

GEORGE Not only is he a highly regarded doctor and a professor of great distinction but he is also a waiter of skill and grace. (*Bows to* HEDDA) Madam.

HEDDA Bertha would have done that.

GEORGE It pleases me to serve you.

HEDDA   Why the two glasses? Mr Loevborg isn't drinking.

GEORGE   One for you. One for Mrs Elvsted.

HEDDA   (*Remembering*) Ah. Just leave it there.

GEORGE   Had you forgotten the woman dedicated-to-her-anxieties? (*To* LOEVBORG) One of the judge's little drolleries.

HEDDA   Can't read your writing, George. What's the name of that village?

GEORGE   Yes — it's called — at the foot of the Brenner Pass — can't read it either — it's called — gone! We spent a night there, remember?

HEDDA   And those three engineers who attached themselves to us after dinner.

GEORGE   The three Spaniards! How could I forget? They couldn't take their eyes off her all night.

HEDDA   Nonsense.

GEORGE   You should have been there, Eilert.

He joins JUDGE BRACK *again.*

LOEVBORG   Just tell me one thing, Hedda —

HEDDA   He's wrong. They were Italian.

LOEVBORG   You did love me, didn't you? Even a little? Even a passing flutter?

HEDDA   Did I? I don't know. We were close friends — I do know that. (*Smiling*) All those secrets you told me — you held nothing back. You told me absolutely everything. Maybe that created the illusion of love.

LOEVBORG   You had to hear everything.

HEDDA   Of course. And at the same time I thought: how courageous of him to be so open. Have you any idea how thrilling it all was for me?

LOEVBORG   We sat on the sofa in the drawing room; the General over at the window with his back to us, reading the newspaper — remember? And we pretended to be engrossed in a magazine — always the same one.

HEDDA   We needed a fascinating honeymoon album.

LOEVBORG   (*Now very softly*) And I told you things about

myself — whispered things that nobody in the world had ever heard. Tales of months lost in an alcoholic fog. Weeks of wilful degradation. Crude, debauched, driven nights. You burrowed into me. You were able to winkle out even the most minute details as if you had some power over me.

HEDDA Had I?

LOEVBORG And those sly questions of yours; never direct; always oblique.

HEDDA But you understood them perfectly.

LOEVBORG Of course I did. But sometimes, when you kept burrowing, insisting on more and more exact detail, I sometimes thought — I used to wonder — how could such a young and sheltered girl, a green child really, how could she be so . . . without shame?

HEDDA My recollection is that you were eager to provide every exact detail, Mr Loevborg.

LOEVBORG We seemed to be altogether alone in the world, isolated in a kind of hothouse intimacy. But wasn't that a sort of love, too? Because when I confessed everything to you, didn't you want to take me in your arms and absolve me and wash me clean? There must have been a kind of love in that, wasn't there?

HEDDA (Dismissively) Nothing at all to do with love.

LOEVBORG Why the relentless interrogation then — that ravenous burrowing? Why?

HEDDA *responds slowly and with consideration.*

HEDDA I was a young girl, an only child. Yes, a green child. I lived with a widowed father in draughty quarters in the centre of an army barrack. I had no relations, no friends, no companions. I knew that on the other side of the barrack wall people were living joyous and exciting lives. And because that life was far beyond my reach I had to have it. And you were my guide around that world because you had experienced it in every extreme. I relished that experience through you, my surrogate out there. All those things I was ravenous to learn, that no one had any suspicion I was hearing, that no green girl ought to hear, I heard it all from you, my mentor. You were my tutor in all the delights and excesses and squalor I might never have known. And I experienced them all through you — in blushing secrecy, in absolute safety.

LOEVBORG But we *were* such friends, Hedda. That friendship should have survived.

HEDDA That was your fault.

LOEVBORG You broke it off.

HEDDA Because you wanted to move it on to a different plane. You misread me, Eilert; I wasn't really without shame. To be shameless required audacity. So I convinced myself that that hothouse intimacy was sufficient for me. And your sudden change — your new demands — terrified me.

LOEVBORG Then why didn't you shoot me when you threatened to? Your father's pistol was still on the table.

HEDDA Cowardice.

LOEVBORG Yes, you are a coward.

HEDDA Terrified of scandal.

LOEVBORG Maybe surrogate living is all you're capable of.

HEDDA So you fled up to Trondheim where the Elvsteds consoled you.

LOEVBORG I can imagine what Thea has told you.

HEDDA Not a word. Have you told Thea about you and me?

LOEVBORG She wouldn't understand. She's a fool.

HEDDA Thea's not a fool.

LOEVBORG Well, foolish about complex things like that.

HEDDA *leans closer to him. Her eyes are on the ground. She speaks softly.*

HEDDA I have something to tell you, Eilert. Not picking up my father's pistol — that wasn't my greatest cowardice that night. A leap with you had to be made; it was time for it. A huge leap for me. And I wanted so much to make it — I can't tell you — so much, so much. But I just couldn't find the courage to take that leap with you.

LOEVBORG I knew that at the time. You had a surfeit of my reports, of a mediated life. You wanted immediate life. (*He catches her hand*) Yes, I knew that then. It's true now, too.

She withdraws her hand very quickly.

HEDDA Careful — that'll do — that's enough — too much.

BERTHA *enters with* MRS ELVSTED. HEDDA *puts the album away, jumps to her feet and flashes a smile.* BERTHA *exits immediately.*

Thea! Come in — come in! Very, very good to see you again.

MRS ELVSTED *bows to* BRACK *and* GEORGE *as she passes them. She and* LOEVBORG *nod to one another.* HEDDA *grips* THEA's *hand.*

THEA Shouldn't I say a word to Mr Tesman?
HEDDA They're happy as they are. And they'll be leaving us soon.
THEA Where are they going?
HEDDA Out on the town. Or to use one of Judge Brack's Americanisms — where does he pick them up? — they're going on the razzle-dazzle.
THEA (*Quickly*) Not you, Eilert?
HEDDA Mr Loevborg is staying here with the prudent women.
THEA I'm so relaxed — so happy — to be here.

THEA *takes a chair to sit beside* LOEVBORG.

HEDDA   No, not there, Thea darling. Sit here (*sofa*) beside
         me. I must be in the centre of things, mustn't I?

THEA   As you wish, Hedda.

LOEVBORG (*To* HEDDA) Isn't she lovely to look at?

HEDDA   (*Stroking* THEA's *hair*) Just to consider?

LOEVBORG Just to contemplate. We are soul-mates, Thea and I.
         We have total trust in one another. We can sit and
         talk with complete openness.

HEDDA   No obliquity?

THEA   (*To* LOEVBORG) I've got to tell Hedda what you say.

LOEVBORG Say about what?

         Pause.

HEDDA   Well?

THEA   (*Softly. To* HEDDA) He says I inspire him.

HEDDA   'Oh my goodness.' And do you? (*To* LOEVBORG)
         Does she?

LOEVBORG She's a very courageous woman.

THEA   Not really.

LOEVBORG When it comes to helping her soul-mate, to battling
         on his behalf, she is altogether without fear.

HEDDA   I envy you. Maybe if I had that sort of courage,
         then perhaps I could manage the business of life
         . . . maybe. (*Sudden change*) Now, Thea, a glass of
         cold punch.

THEA   Not for me, thanks. I never touch alcohol.

HEDDA   Mr Loevborg?

LOEVBORG Nothing for me either.

THEA   He's fine, Hedda.

LOEVBORG We're a pair of killjoys.

HEDDA   But if I wanted you to?

LOEVBORG Why would that make a difference?

HEDDA   So I have no power over you at all?

LOEVBORG Not in this matter.

HEDDA   Well, I think you should have a glass.

THEA   Hedda!

HEDDA   For your own sake.

LOEVBORG I don't know what that means.

HEDDA   And to perplex other people —

LOEVBORG   Who?

HEDDA   — who might suspect that in your heart of hearts you aren't as assured as you appear, that you're quite irresolute in fact.

THEA   Oh, Hedda, no!

HEDDA   To confound them.

LOEVBORG   Let them suspect what they like.

THEA   He's right. Who cares about them?

HEDDA   I could see it in the judge just now, how scornful he was when he saw you were afraid to join them in a drink.

LOEVBORG   I wanted to stay here and talk to you.

HEDDA   'Only cold punch, man. It's not poison.' And when you didn't dare go to their stupid party I saw him winking at George.

LOEVBORG   (*Very controlled*) I didn't dare?

HEDDA   That's what the shrewd judge thought.

LOEVBORG   (*Shrugs*) Who cares what he thinks.

HEDDA   So you're not going with them?

LOEVBORG   Haven't I already said I'm staying here with you and Thea?

HEDDA   Good.

LOEVBORG   What's got into you, Hedda?

HEDDA   (*Quickly, sharply*) What do you mean by that?

LOEVBORG   I don't know what's going on here. I was invited to a dinner party. I said no. I was offered a glass of cold port. I said no. Can I be any more explicit?

HEDDA   You're a man of iron discipline. Altogether admirable. (*She strokes* THEA's *cheek*) Thea tells us you're . . . impeccable.

THEA   (*Confused*) Hedda, what are you — ?

HEDDA   And she's right. The peccable Eilert that I admired belongs to the past. That's what I tried to tell you this morning. But nothing would convince her you weren't already off on the 'razzle-dazzle'. As Eilert says, you're a very silly woman.

THEA   (*Shocked*) Eilert — ? You two were talking about me behind — ?

HEDDA Consider him, Thea. Is that a man on the verge of collapsing again? You're still not anxious for him, are you?

LOEVBORG Something *has* got into you.

THEA Hedda, dear God, Hedda, what are you trying to do?

HEDDA Keep your voice down. That awful judge is listening.

LOEVBORG (*To* THEA) Anxious for me, were you?

THEA (*About to cry*) Oh my God . . .

LOEVBORG And in panic? Your faith in me is moving. (*To* THEA) To your great belief in me.

He picks up a glass and drinks it quickly.

THEA (*To* HEDDA) This is what you wanted to happen, isn't it?

LOEVBORG And to Mrs Tesman and her ugly manipulations.

He begins to fill the glass again. HEDDA *restrains him.*

HEDDA That's enough. You've a dinner party to go to.

THEA He's not going to that, Hedda!

HEDDA Quiet. You're being watched.

LOEVBORG *puts the glass down.*

LOEVBORG Tell me truthfully, Thea: did your husband know you followed me here?

THEA Oh, Hedda . . .

LOEVBORG Was it agreed between you and the resident magistrate that you would come and spy on me? He wasn't genuinely concerned for his children's tutor, was he? Or did he just want me back to make up his card school?

THEA (*Now crying*) Eilert, please, Eilert . . .

LOEVBORG *raises the glass again.*

LOEVBORG To the resident magistrate and his obedient wife.

Again HEDDA *stops him.*

HEDDA I've said that's enough. You've promised to read part of your book to George.

He is suddenly calm and controlled again.

LOEVBORG You're so right. I'm sorry, Thea. Pardon your soul-mate. I'm really sorry. No need for anxiety — I'll be fine. Don't panic. Remember: you *have* rescued me. We both believe that. I'll be just fine. Promise.

THEA I know you will. I trust you totally.

BRACK *and* GEORGE *come down to the drawing room.*

BRACK Time for us to leave, Mrs Tesman.

HEDDA So soon?

BRACK Dionysus is getting impatient.

LOEVBORG (*Suddenly*) Count me in!

THEA (*In panic*) Eilert! Eilert Loevborg — !

HEDDA (*Squeezing her arm*) Control yourself.

BRACK (*To* LOEVBORG) You know you may be exposing yourself to a minor misconduct?

LOEVBORG (*Laughs*) May I, please?

BRACK (*Quietly, to* GEORGE) I did confess my unease with the Saint Paul canard, didn't I?

GEORGE (*Laughs*) Judge Brack!

BRACK Not converted. Concussed by the fall from his horse.

LOEVBORG (*Picking up his manuscript. To* GEORGE) A few chapters I'd like to show you before it goes off to the publisher.

GEORGE I can't wait. Hold on — how is Mrs Elvsted to get home?

LOEVBORG I'll see Mrs Elvsted home. Who else? About ten o'clock, Mrs Tesman — will that suit you?

HEDDA Perfect.

GEORGE I'm afraid I may not be back by ten, Hedda. What do you think, Judge?

BRACK A.m. or p.m.?

HEDDA (*Caution*) Judge!

BRACK Depends on how successful we are at razzling-dazzling. Or is it razzle-dazzling? Or razzling-dazzle?

HEDDA Don't rush home on my account.

GEORGE Ten o'clock, Eilert?

LOEVBORG On the dot.

THEA Promise, Eilert?

BRACK Never exact a promise. Like the oath in court, nobody trusts it for a second.

HEDDA I'd give a lot to be a fly on your wall, Judge.

BRACK Not advisable. You might see things not at all suitable for a mind of such manifest innocence.

GEORGE Ten o'clock, Thea?

THEA Please.

> BRACK, GEORGE *and* LOEVBORG *all leave.* BERTHA *enters and lights a lamp. She then clears away the glasses.*

What will happen, Hedda?

HEDDA What will happen is that he will come home — when he comes home — with a wreath of vine leaves in his damp hair; gleaming, triumphant, exuding power.

THEA He will look after himself, won't he?

HEDDA He'll be his own master again — a free man again.

THEA Oh God, I hope he is alright.

HEDDA I don't doubt him. My faith in the real Eilert Loevborg is absolute. Which of us will be proved right, Thea?

THEA You're after something, Hedda. What are you after?

> *Brief pause.*

HEDDA   For once in my life I want control over the destiny
         of a man.
THEA   You already have that power. You have George.
HEDDA   (*Laughs*) Don't be stupid. Who would want to shape
         that fate? Don't you appreciate, sweet little Thea,
         how poor and disadvantaged I am and how opulent
         and privileged you are? (*She suddenly embraces her*)
         There's a whiff of expectancy in the atmosphere.
         Don't you smell it? I think I'll set fire to your hair
         after all.

         THEA *jumps up.*

THEA   Let me go! Let go of me! You terrify me, Hedda!

         BERTHA *enters.*

BERTHA   I've laid the tea things in the dining room.
HEDDA   Good. We're coming.
THEA   I'm going home, Hedda — now — by myself.
         Sorry. I can't stay here. I'm too scared of —
HEDDA   Oh shut up, you fool! You're going to have supper
         first with terrifying Hedda. And then — then Eilert
         Loevborg will come. With a crown of vine leaves in
         his damp hair.

         Quick black.

ACT THREE

Dawn, the following day. The curtains are closed. The lamp is turned low and still burning. HEDDA, *fully dressed, is asleep on the sofa. She is covered by a rug.* THEA *is in an armchair beside the stove, her feet on a stool, a large shawl around her shoulders.*

A noise off. THEA *sits up suddenly and listens intently, then sinks back again.*

THEA Oh my God, no . . .

BERTHA *enters on tiptoe.*

What was that?

BERTHA A girl came with this letter.

THEA (*Holds out her hand*) Thank you, Bertha.

BERTHA It's for Dr Tesman, ma'am.

THEA Ah.

BERTHA From his aunt, Miss Juliana. That big rough lump of a maid of hers brought it. I'll leave it here (*table*) for him. Better put that lamp out. Beginning to smoke.

THEA It'll soon be daylight.

BERTHA It's daylight already, ma'am.

She turns the lamp off.

THEA Still no sign of the men?

BERTHA You might have known. Once they fell in with that certain gentleman there was bound to be bother. We all know his pedigree.

THEA You'll waken Mrs Tesman.

BERTHA Will I put some wood on the stove?

THEA Not for me, thank you. The room's quite warm.

BERTHA *exits. The noise wakens* HEDDA.

HEDDA What's that?
 THEA Bertha, the maid.
HEDDA (*Stretching*) What time is it, Thea?
 THEA After seven.
HEDDA When did George get home?
 THEA He's not back yet. Nobody's back yet.
HEDDA And we sat up like fools till four!
 THEA You had a good sleep.
HEDDA I had. And you?
 THEA Not a wink.
HEDDA Didn't even doze?
 THEA I had a miserable night.

HEDDA *goes to her.*

HEDDA I know . . . I know . . . But there is nothing to worry
       about. I know only too well what happened.
 THEA What?
HEDDA They had a very heavy night at the judge's.
 THEA (*Anxiously*) Did they?
HEDDA It's always much worse than they expect. And
       George didn't dare face in here in that condition in
       the middle of the night. So off he went to the aunts
       — they keep his old room for him.
 THEA No, he's not there. A letter came from there just now.
HEDDA (*Picks up the letter*) Ah — Aunt Juliana's handwriting.
       Then he's still at Judge Brack's.
 THEA You know very well they're not still at the judge's
       home, Hedda.
HEDDA Thea darling, you look completely washed out.
 THEA I am.
HEDDA Then go upstairs to my bedroom and lie down.
       First on the right at the top of the stairs. A sleep
       will restore you.
 THEA I couldn't sleep, Hedda. I'll wait until George comes
       back and he'll know where —
HEDDA I'll call you the moment he comes. There is no point

in sitting up here — now is there?

THEA You're right, I suppose.

HEDDA You *will* sleep.

THEA And you'll call me?

HEDDA Promise.

THEA For a short while then.

> THEA *exits.* HEDDA *pulls back the curtains and the room is flooded with morning sunshine. She takes a hand-mirror from the drawer of the desk, examines her face, deftly arranges her hair. Then she rings the bell for* BERTHA. BERTHA *enters.*

HEDDA You let the fire die. The room's freezing.

BERTHA I offered to —

HEDDA Put some logs on now.

BERTHA Yes, ma'am.

> *The doorbell rings.*

HEDDA Answer that. I'll look after the stove.

> HEDDA *kneels in front of the stove.* GEORGE *enters. He tries to tiptoe soundlessly up to the back room.*

(*Not looking up*) Good morning.

GEORGE (*Loud and breezy*) Hedda! Good morning to you, too. You're up early. I thought you'd still be asleep.

HEDDA No need to shout. Mrs Elvsted's up in my bed.

GEORGE She spent the night here?

HEDDA None of you gentlemen remembered to take her home, did you?

GEORGE I know. Sorry about that. The thought did come into my head a few times during the night but between one thing and another . . .

> HEDDA *closes the door of the stove and stands up.*

HEDDA Well, had you a good time?

GEORGE Were you worried about me?

HEDDA I asked had you a good time.

GEORGE Yes. I suppose so. The usual. (*Laughs*) At one point in the night the judge announced he was getting too old for 'making whoopee'. He says that's a Navaho-Indian expression.

HEDDA Did Eilert Loevborg behave himself?

GEORGE For a full hour he read to me from his new book. In the judge's breakfast room. Just the two of us alone there together. I was mesmerized, Hedda. For a full hour.

HEDDA *sits at the table.*

HEDDA Well, aren't you going to tell me about it?

Pause.

GEORGE It is just amazing, Hedda. Eilert Loevborg has written an amazing book. What can I tell you? Utterly amazing.

HEDDA (*Coldly*) So Mr Loevborg's book amazed you.

GEORGE Probably the most remarkable book I've ever read! The clarity, the insights, the poise — I can't think of any book that had such a profound impact on me.

HEDDA 'Oh my goodness.'

GEORGE And as I listened to him reading, Hedda, I must confess I had the strangest experience. I was astounded by the book — of course, of course I was; overawed by it. But at the same time a portion of me stayed very cool and very analytical. And I suddenly knew I was jealous of Eilert Loevborg. I thought: it's a bit unfair, isn't it, that a man so weak and so damaged should have been endowed with this enormous talent. He doesn't value it. He has no real interest in it. He's not capable of protecting and nurturing it. That's a little unfair, isn't it?

HEDDA Is it?

GEORGE It is. Because for all his genius he just can't cope.

HEDDA   Cope with what? Mediocrity? The second-rate?

GEORGE Just with being alive, I suppose. Maybe just . . . living is beyond him.

HEDDA   Many people have that problem. That doesn't mean he's damaged. Anyhow, how did the night end?

GEORGE I'm afraid the night just . . . disintegrated. Dionysian, I'm sorry to say.

HEDDA   Did he have vine leaves in his hair?

GEORGE (*Puzzled*) Eilert? No, I don't recall vine leaves. No, he was wearing a tweed cap. Yes, a brown tweed cap. I remember him holding it against his chest when he delivered this long oration about the splendid woman who inspired him to write the book.

HEDDA   Thea?

GEORGE Addicted-to-her-anxieties Thea, as the judge calls her. He didn't name her but we all knew who he meant. And that was the word he used, Hedda — 'inspired'!

HEDDA   Drunken blether. When did you break up?

GEORGE I've no idea what time it was. We all left the judge's place together. Brack came some of the way with us — to clear his head. Poor old Eilert was in bits: we almost had to carry him.

HEDDA   (*Ironically*) Never!

GEORGE And then a strange thing happened. No, not a strange thing; a very funny thing. No, not a funny thing at all; actually a tragic thing. No, no, that's too strong. A sad thing, yes; yes, a very sad thing happened.

HEDDA   (*Exaggerated patience*) What happened, George?

GEORGE The others were in front of me. I had fallen a little behind. I ran to catch up with them. And what do you think I found lying at the side of the road?

HEDDA   (*Crossly*) Please.

GEORGE You mustn't tell a soul, Hedda; for Eilert's sake. Promise me that.

He produces a large envelope from the pocket of his

overcoat — the manuscript.

HEDDA Not the 'amazing' new book?

GEORGE Yes.

HEDDA The one he read to you for an hour last night?

GEORGE Yes.

HEDDA The manuscript he had here yesterday?

GEORGE Yes.

HEDDA He wasn't aware he had lost it?

GEORGE No.

HEDDA Why didn't you give it back to him there and then?

GEORGE In the state he was in!

HEDDA You didn't tell any of the others?

GEORGE I felt I oughtn't to — for Eilert's sake.

HEDDA So nobody knows you have it?

GEORGE And nobody's going to know. I'll give it to him later today when he has sobered up.

HEDDA How was he when you saw him last?

GEORGE Almost footless. In the centre of town. But determined not to let the night end. That's when we all broke up. The judge disappeared somewhere. A couple of us bribed a night watchman to share his poisonous coffee with us. Two others went off somewhere with Eilert: they told me they were bringing him home but they were going in the wrong direction! All very messy. I'm feeling a little fragile — would you mind if I lay down for an hour? Then I'll go to Eilert's.

He picks up the manuscript.

HEDDA Let me read it first.

GEORGE Oh, Hedda, you couldn't do that.

HEDDA Couldn't or daren't?

GEORGE Wouldn't it be a little . . . intrusive? I mean it's very personal to him; like a diary. And when he wakes up and finds it gone, can you imagine the panic he'll be in?

HEDDA He can rewrite it, can't he?

GEORGE I wouldn't think so. Something as unique as that can be produced only under a great urgency of inspiration. Wouldn't you agree?

HEDDA I wouldn't know. I'm not a great writer like you people. By the way — a letter for you.

He examines the envelope.

GEORGE Auntie Juju's writing.

He leaves the manuscript on the stool and sits to read the letter.

I love her handwriting; it's so resolute . . . Oh my God, Hedda, Auntie Rena's dying! Oh my God!

HEDDA You expected that, didn't you?

GEORGE I'm to go at once if I hope to see her. Of course I do! Of course I will! Poor, poor Auntie Rena. I never expected this — not really. I'll go straight away. Come with me, Hedda, will you, please?

HEDDA No, no, don't ask that of me.

GEORGE But Hedda, love —

HEDDA Please, George.

GEORGE You won't have a chance to see her again.

HEDDA I couldn't face it. I couldn't look at her. Don't ask that of me, George. No, no, I can't look at anything at all like that. Please.

GEORGE I see . . . (*Sudden panic*) Where's my coat? My hat? In the hall! Don't need gloves, do I? — it's September, isn't it? — I hope I'll make it in time.

BERTHA *enters.*

BERTHA Excuse me, Doctor —

GEORGE Auntie Rena's dying, Bertha.

BERTHA Oh mother of God!

GEORGE Our lovely Auntie Rena's slipping away.

BERTHA Mother of God, my lovely Miss Rena.

GEORGE I'm on my way over. I'll bring her your love.

BERTHA Yes, yes, Georgie! All my love! Mother of God, my lovely Miss Rena — oh sweet mother of God.

BERTHA *begins to cry.*

HEDDA What is it you want?
BERTHA What's that?
HEDDA Do you want something?
BERTHA Judge Brack is here.
GEORGE What the hell's Brack doing here at this moment? I can't see him now.
HEDDA I can. Tell him to come in.

As BERTHA *leaves, sobbing,* GEORGE *goes to her and catches her elbow.*

GEORGE I know. Thank you, Bertha. I know. Our lovely Miss Rena. Thank you. (*To* HEDDA) I'll slip out this way.
HEDDA The manuscript, George.
GEORGE Yes, give it to me.
HEDDA Why would you take it to your aunts'? I'll look after it here.
GEORGE You're right. Of course. Good. I'm off.

He exits. HEDDA *places the manuscript in the bookcase above the desk.* BRACK *enters.*

BRACK I know — I know — an unconscionable hour again. It's becoming a sad little habit. Why can't I discipline myself to stay away?
HEDDA You just missed George. His Aunt Rena is dying.
BRACK Ah, melancholy tidings. Such honourable girls, those Tesman ladies. George will be perturbed.
HEDDA Probably. I gather last night's party was . . . robust?
BRACK Is that the verdict? Verging on the turbulent, I'd suggest. (*He opens his coat*) Haven't had time to change — that's the telltale. Did Tesman enjoy himself?
HEDDA What did he tell me? Eilert Loevborg declared that

his new book was 'inspired' by the anxious Thea?

BRACK He did indeed — solemnly.

HEDDA Judge Brack declared he is getting too old for 'making whoopee'?

BRACK He did indeed — jestingly. Do you know what making whoopee means?

HEDDA No.

BRACK I tell myself it's an American-Indian word for making love. And if it is I'm not too old at all. In fact, elegant Hedda, I'm only approaching my peak.

HEDDA (*Laughs*) And George and two others cadged bad coffee from a night watchman.

BRACK Loevborg wasn't one of the two?

HEDDA No. George thought Loevborg had gone home at that stage.

BRACK Decent, credulous, trusting George. That's what they wanted him to believe. Have you any idea where Loevborg and his two friends spent the residue of the night?

HEDDA Why do I expect somewhere improper?

BRACK Because you're a very naughty woman, thank heavens. And you're so right. I knew Loevborg had got an invitation earlier in the day. But he declined because — as we all assumed — he is . . . 'delivered'?

HEDDA Saved, Judge.

> BRACK *crosses his arms in front of his face to ward off evil — as he did before.*

BRACK Please! So he resisted the invite with valiance until alcohol undermined him, and himself and the others ended up in the establishment of a Mademoiselle Circe.

HEDDA Circe?

BRACK A pseudonym. Yes, a little flamboyant. But then she is a lady with classical inclinations as well.

HEDDA A sort of singer-dancer?

BRACK Among other accomplishments.

HEDDA Red haired?

BRACK You've heard of her then?

HEDDA She carries a revolver in her handbag.

BRACK That I didn't know. So you and she share a passion for artillery? Yes, some years ago Mademoiselle Circe was up before me on some charge or other. In those days her more decorous name was Mary Bridget O'Donnell. Eilert Loevborg was a client of hers back then, too. (*Trying to remember*) What was the charge? Yes, cruelty to animals. Surely there's no connection between that and her profession?

HEDDA And last night ended badly?

BRACK And it began with amity and protestations of affection. Ended very badly indeed. Loevborg accused Circe of larceny. Circe replied with a smackeroo on the kisser: smackeroo — thump; kisser — (*He points to his mouth*)

HEDDA What had she stolen?

BRACK Both Americanisms. Stolen? — his wallet, some coins, and some other important possessions — or so he insists. There was an exchange of blows — yes, male and female. And blood was drawn. Sordid. Anyhow Loevborg was arrested and removed to the police station where he was most truculent: lacerated a young officer's uniform and then rendered him horizontal. The police are my source of all this squalid information. As I say sometimes when I'm on the bench and wish to sound impressively judicial, I say: How can civilized people sink so low?

HEDDA So there were no vine leaves in his hair?

BRACK No. Not mentioned in the police report. They know, of course, that he spent the early part of the evening at my house. That could be embarrassing for me.

HEDDA He'll be up in court then?

BRACK Probably. And you could well be caught up in the embarrassment.

HEDDA How?

BRACK He is a guest here. As we talk, his 'inspiration' sleeps upstairs, Bertha tells me. And Mrs Elvsted won't be returning to the resident magistrate in the near future.

HEDDA There are many places she and Loevborg can meet.

BRACK No respectable house in this city will welcome them from now on.

HEDDA Including this respectable house?

BRACK I would hope so. I would be quite displeased if Eilert Loevborg were welcome here. If I were to discover that he was intruding —

HEDDA On the triangle?

BRACK That would be like losing a home.

HEDDA You want to be the only rooster in the yard?

BRACK Of course. And I shall fight for that in every way I know how, lovely Hedda; every way.

HEDDA (*Uneasily*) You are a dangerous man, Judge Brack.

BRACK (*Pretended hurt*) I'm not — am I?

HEDDA Thank goodness you haven't any kind of hold over me.

BRACK No, not now.

HEDDA Do I detect a threat there?

BRACK Hedda! The triangle can flourish only with mutual consent. Compulsion would poison the benign atmosphere. And now I must depart. And please do something about a crack in the door of your bedroom: you know how I adore contemplating you.

HEDDA You're going out through the garden?

BRACK Shorter, isn't it?

HEDDA And devious.

BRACK You mean devious as in *de via*, off the main track, don't you?

HEDDA Do I?

BRACK I think so. A woman like you knows that following an erratic course can be exciting.

HEDDA So can firing a pistol.

BRACK (*Laughs*) Thank heavens people don't shoot tame roosters.

HEDDA Especially when they've got only one.

They both laugh as he exits. She shuts the French windows behind him and watches him as he leaves. Then she goes to the desk and takes the manuscript from the bookcase. She begins to read it but stops when she hears raised voices in the hall. She listens for a few seconds, puts the manuscript in the drawer of the desk and locks it.

BERTHA (*Off*) You're not going in there, sir!

LOEVBORG (*Off*) Out of my way, woman!

BERTHA (*Off*) Take your dirty hands off me!

LOEVBORG (*Off*) I am going in! Out of my way! Let me pass!

The door is flung open. LOEVBORG *bursts in. His hair is wild, his clothes dishevelled and he has a small plaster on his lip. When he sees* HEDDA *he makes an effort to control himself and bows to her.*

HEDDA So Mr Loevborg has finally turned up. A little late to take Thea home, isn't it?

LOEVBORG I know. I'm sorry. And forgive this (*appearance*) . . .

HEDDA How did you know she's still here?

LOEVBORG I went to her lodgings. They said she hadn't returned.

HEDDA And were they surprised?

LOEVBORG At what?

HEDDA Didn't they think it strange that you called?

LOEVBORG That this dishevelled creature was looking for her? If they did, they gave no indication. George isn't up yet?

HEDDA Not yet.

LOEVBORG When did he get home?

HEDDA Very late.

LOEVBORG What did he tell you about last night?

HEDDA It was the usual disgraceful affair at the judge's.

LOEVBORG Nothing else?

HEDDA I don't remember. I was half asleep.

THEA ELVSTED *runs in from the back room and goes*

straight to LOEVBORG. *She catches both his hands in hers and her eyes search his face anxiously.*

THEA Eilert! Oh Eilert! At last! Give me your hands! What happened to your face? The patient hands are so cold. Is your jacket torn? You're very pale, Eilert — are you alright?

LOEVBORG Too late, Thea. Finished.

THEA Too late? What's too late? What's finished?

LOEVBORG I'm washed up. It's all over. I've come to the end.

THEA I will not listen to —

LOEVBORG When you've heard what happened last night you'll —

THEA I don't care what happened last night. Last night's over. We've had these setbacks before and we struggled through and triumphed.

HEDDA I'll leave you two alone.

LOEVBORG No, stay, please.

THEA Today is a new day, Eilert. Today you'll make a fresh beginning.

LOEVBORG I'm not talking about last night's party. I'm talking about you and me, Thea. We're finished, too.

THEA Finished? Eilert, we —

LOEVBORG We mustn't see each other again.

THEA Hedda, tell him to —

LOEVBORG I don't need you any more. I don't mean to sound so brutal. But the working partnership we had is finished.

THEA You're upset, Eilert. Something happened last night that —

LOEVBORG Listen to what I'm saying to you. I'm never going to write ever again. My life is over. All done with. So is our work together, our working partnership — that's over, too.

THEA But we're collaborators, Eilert, soul-mates —

LOEVBORG Finished. Completely finished. So what you must do is expel me and all that past from your head — completely.

THEA He doesn't mean it, Hedda?

LOEVBORG And begin to assemble a new life for yourself.

THEA That's not possible.

LOEVBORG You're a young woman, you're very competent, everything is still very possible for you. Go back to Trondheim and your family and —

THEA Never that! Can't do that! Oh Eilert! I don't believe that that's all it was to you — a working partnership. I know it was much, much richer than that. I know it was. Have you any idea what you're doing to me? You can't discard me like that. You are my life, Eilert; the only life I have. I don't exist unless I'm with you. You *do* know that, don't you? And I have got to be with you when the new book comes out, Eilert, our book, yours and mine. I do have that right. Because it is ours, Eilert. We are its parents.

LOEVBORG We were.

THEA And I have got to witness the happiness on your face, and the delight and satisfaction of hearing people applaud you and praise you and lay before you all the honour and respect you have always deserved. Because it will be an occasion of such joy for us, Eilert. Yes, of course it will be a literary event too — 'significant' and 'ground-breaking'. But for us — for you and for me — it will be just so joyous, just so happy, just such a private and intense celebration. Oh Eilert, I have got to be there to share that happiness with you. Even just to witness it. And to see that old Eilert Loevborg — that damaged, hesitant, apologetic, irresolute, flinching Eilert Loevborg — to have him exorcised forever. You can understand that, can't you?

LOEVBORG There won't be a book launch, Thea. There can't be a book launch. There is no book.

THEA I don't understand what —

LOEVBORG There is no longer a book to launch.

THEA Of course there is a book, Eilert. We laboured over it for eighteen months. And when we were finished I wrote out the entire manuscript myself in my own hand.

LOEVBORG That manuscript is torn up, Thea.

THEA Torn up?

LOEVBORG I destroyed that manuscript; tore it up; into shreds.

THEA But Eilert —

LOEVBORG That manuscript doesn't exist any more.

THEA (*Now accepting — and stunned*) Oh no, noooo . . .

HEDDA (*Involuntarily*) But that's not —

LOEVBORG Not true, you think?

HEDDA If you say it is . . .

LOEVBORG I've destroyed my life. Why not my work?

THEA Why would he want to hurt me, Hedda? Tell me it's a lie, Hedda, isn't it?

LOEVBORG I ripped it into a thousand pieces and threw them into the fjord. They floated for a short time and then sank — just like myself.

THEA It's the truth, Hedda. He's telling us the awful truth.

HEDDA Yes.

THEA You have torn up a life, Eilert. You know that?

LOEVBORG I know that.

THEA Destroyed a life I helped to create.

LOEVBORG Yes.

THEA Destroyed our child, Eilert Loevborg — you know that. And part of me will be mourning for the rest of my days.

HEDDA Maybe you should —

THEA I think I will go now, Hedda.

HEDDA Back to your lodgings?

THEA My coat and hat are probably on the hallstand. To my lodgings? No, not there; not back to Trondheim. No idea where I'm going, Hedda. No idea at all. I think I'll just wander . . . until the earth goes still again.

She exits. We hear the front door shut. Pause.

HEDDA Aren't you going to take her to her lodgings?

LOEVBORG She's better not seen with me.

HEDDA Can't you see she's shattered, Eilert?

LOEVBORG   For a time. Never underestimate Mrs Elvsted: she's
a resilient woman.

HEDDA   What happened last night that was so irrevocable?

LOEVBORG   Oh, I began all over again last night: back to the old
treadmill, Hedda. The drinking. The whoring. The
brawling. And the curse of it is that I don't have
the stomach for it now. Even as I crave it and find
satisfaction, it nauseates me. That can end in only
one way. In the old days I spat in the face of the
world with such easy defiance. So in that she
certainly succeeded: she broke my courage; she
fractured my will.

HEDDA   (*As though to herself*) Silly little bitch. Yet somehow
she has shaped a man's destiny. (*To* LOEVBORG) You
were brutal to her, Eilert.

LOEVBORG   She had to look at what had happened.

HEDDA   A part of her *will* be in mourning for the rest of her
days.

LOEVBORG   For God's sake! For all of a week — maybe!

HEDDA   To destroy the one thing in her life that she believed
made that life cohere — isn't that cruel?

LOEVBORG   I will tell you the truth, Hedda.

HEDDA   About what?

LOEVBORG   Promise me you won't breathe a word of this to
Thea.

HEDDA   What are you talking about?

LOEVBORG   The manuscript. Promise.

HEDDA   Promise — promise.

LOEVBORG   I didn't tear it up and throw the pieces in the fjord.
But I did defile it.

HEDDA   I don't understand what —

LOEVBORG   Sullied it — contaminated it — betrayed it.

HEDDA   But you still have it.

LOEVBORG   Thea said it was like killing our child. But there are
other obscene things a father may do to his child
that may be just as evil. Suppose a man comes
home in the early hours of the morning and says to
the mother of his child, 'I have been out brawling
and drinking and whoring all night long. And I

had our child with me in all of those dens. He watched the brawling and the drinking and he witnessed the whoring. And now our child is lost. I can't find him. I don't know what hands he has fallen into or where they are holding him or what those hands are doing to him.'

HEDDA   It's not a child, Eilert. It's a book — a book.

LOEVBORG   Thea's soul was in that book.

HEDDA   I know all that but —

LOEVBORG   She made it her whole life. That book was the repository of all her hopes and aspirations. It was her pure heart that gave that book its shape and quickened it. How can I look into her pure face ever again? I can't — can I?

Pause.

HEDDA   Where will you go?

LOEVBORG   That doesn't matter now. (*Pause*) Put an end to the whole squalid business.

HEDDA   You mean that?

LOEVBORG   Yes.

HEDDA   You've made your mind up?

LOEVBORG   Yes.

HEDDA   When?

LOEVBORG   (*Shrugs*) Soon.

HEDDA   Listen to me, Eilert Loevborg. If you do it, when you do it, do it as beautifully as you can.

LOEVBORG   (*Smiles*) Beautifully? You mean with vine leaves in my hair?

HEDDA   (*Slowly. With deliberation*) No, none of that nonsense any more. But with beauty. One beautiful gesture, Eilert Loevborg — a gesture that becomes you. Please. (*Pause*) And now you must go. Don't come back here again. Goodbye, Eilert Loevborg.

LOEVBORG   Adieu, Hedda Gabler. Give George Tesman my best wishes.

He turns to go.

HEDDA Wait. A souvenir to take with you.

> *She unlocks the desk where she has the manuscript. She takes out the pistol case. She removes one of the pistols and hands it to him.*

LOEVBORG This is my souvenir?
HEDDA Don't you recognize it? I aimed it at you once long ago.
LOEVBORG You should have used it then.
HEDDA It might be useful now.

> LOEVBORG *takes it and puts it in his breast pocket.*

LOEVBORG Thank you.
HEDDA (*As he leaves*) And with beauty, Eilert Loevborg. Give me that promise. One beautiful, final gesture. A final gesture that becomes you.

> *She goes to the drawer again and takes out the manuscript. She goes to the armchair beside the stove. She sits there with the manuscript on her lap. Now she opens the envelope, pulls out some pages and looks at them. Now she opens the door of the stove and slowly feeds the pages into the flames. As she does:*

HEDDA This is your child I'm burning, Thea; anxious Thea, Thea with ridiculous golden curls. I'm burning the child you had by him. I'm burning your baby, Thea, your and Eilert Loevborg's baby.

> *Fade to black. End of Act Three.*

ACT FOUR

That same night. The drawing room is in darkness. The back room is lit by a lamp hanging above the table. The curtains are pulled across the French windows. HEDDA, *dressed in black, paces restlessly round the drawing room. Now she goes up to the back room and plays a few rapid chords on the piano. Now she returns to the drawing room and to her pacing.*

BERTHA *enters with a lighted lamp. She has been crying and has black ribbons in her cap. She places the lamp on the drawing-room table.*

HEDDA That lamp is dangerous. Turn the wick down. (*Pause*) What's your name again?

BERTHA Bertha.

HEDDA That wick's too high. (*Pause*) I'm talking to you, Berna.

BERTHA I hear you.

HEDDA That wick is dangerous. Turn it down.

> BERTHA *does not obey her. She stares at* HEDDA *for a few seconds — a mixture of grief and sullenness and defiance — and shuffles off.*

(*To herself*) Sullen bitch.

> JULIANA, *dressed in mourning clothes, enters.* HEDDA *goes to her with her hands outstretched.*

JULIANA She's gone, Hedda. It's all over.

HEDDA I know.

JULIANA Our lovely Rena has left us.

HEDDA George sent me a quick note.

JULIANA He said he would but I thought I must tell Hedda

84

myself.

HEDDA Thank you.

JULIANA She went so quickly in the end. I just wish she could have chosen a different time to leave us. Hedda's home is a house of happy expectation just now. It shouldn't be overcast by death.

HEDDA And it was a peaceful end?

JULIANA Very peaceful. And after a life of suffering borne with such fortitude, that was becoming, wasn't it? She kissed me; and she kissed Georgie; and she said she was sorry she would miss a new birthday blossom on his slippers next month — she had planned to do a Flower of Bethlehem. Then she asked was Bertha not there and she sent her her special love. Then she sighed once — a mere hint of impatience; just once. And she was gone. It was very beautiful. (*Suddenly brisk*) He's not home yet?

HEDDA He said he might be delayed. Take a seat, Miss Tesman.

JULIANA Thank you, Hedda dear, but I must run. I have to call on the undertaker. And I must do her hair myself: I want her to look really beautiful. She was quite vain about her hair, little Miss Rena, when she was young; such a mass of curls.

HEDDA Can I help in any way?

JULIANA I wouldn't hear of it. We can't have Hedda Tesman turning her hand to that kind of work: her thoughts are on happier events, thank goodness. I really must go, Hedda. I still have to sew up Rena's shroud. But it won't be long until there'll be joyous sewing to be done for this house, will it? (*Whispers*) Aren't you thrilled? I can't wait.

GEORGE *enters from the hall. He seems disoriented.*

HEDDA (*Sharply*) You took your time.

GEORGE Sorry — sorry. Auntie Juju, hello! Didn't know you were here. Did you tell me you were coming? Sorry — I'm a little confused.

JULIANA Did you get all those messages done?

GEORGE Most of them. I couldn't remember some of them. Could you write them down for me?

JULIANA *catches his elbow.*

JULIANA I understand of course, Georgie.

GEORGE The old head's just a bit addled today.

JULIANA I know. It's all very sad. But it's a relief, too. You mustn't go under. There are so many arrangements to be made.

GEORGE Are there?

JULIANA Small things, yes; dozens of them.

GEORGE (*Now totally confused*) What do you mean it's a relief?

JULIANA For lovely Aunt Rena, Georgie!

GEORGE Ah. Yes.

HEDDA (*Covering*) You'll miss her terribly, Miss Tesman.

JULIANA We all will. But we must rise above. Immediately after the funeral the first thing I'm going to do is get somebody for her little room. Somebody about her age; bedridden, too. There'll be plenty of applicants, I'm sure.

HEDDA You're going to take on that burden again — and a total stranger?

JULIANA That's not a burden, Hedda. I need someone to live for. Thinking only of yourself and your problems can be very boring and very unhealthy. And please God there'll soon be work in this house that an old aunt can lend a hand with.

HEDDA (*Quickly*) We've got to talk about that Berna creature.

GEORGE Bertha? What about Bertha?

HEDDA She's becoming intolerable.

JULIANA I'm sure she's not herself today, Hedda. She devoted her entire life to Auntie Rena. Try to be patient with her for the time being, will you? I'll speak to her later. (*As she leaves*) Such a peculiar thought came into my head as I was coming here tonight. I thought: Rena is still here with us in her own little room; but she's also with your father, dear Joachim. Isn't that strange?

GEORGE (*Flatly*) Amazing, Auntie Juju, yes.

JULIANA She'll be telling him about your doctorate and all the ins and outs of the professorship. And most important of all, Hedda — your good news! I'll see myself out. Let Bertha get over these difficult days. I'll have a word with her then.

She exits.

GEORGE Your good news, she said?

HEDDA Oh shut up! What's the matter with you today?

GEORGE It's Eilert, Hedda. Can't get him out of my head. I'm so worried about him. I'm afraid he might do himself an injury.

HEDDA Why do you say that?

GEORGE Well, I dropped into his lodgings just to reassure him that the manuscript was safe here. But he wasn't there. Then I bumped into Thea down at the harbour. She seemed to be very distressed. She told me Eilert had been here this morning.

HEDDA Just after you left.

GEORGE And that he announced he'd torn the manuscript into pieces. He didn't say that, did he?

HEDDA He did.

GEORGE He must be demented. Why wouldn't he be? But you told him we have it?

HEDDA No.

GEORGE You didn't?!

HEDDA Did you tell Thea?

GEORGE You should have told him, Hedda. The poor creature might do something desperate.

HEDDA Did you tell Thea?

GEORGE No. Give me the envelope. I'll try his lodgings again.

HEDDA The envelope is gone.

GEORGE Gone where?

HEDDA I burned it.

GEORGE Eilert's manuscript?

HEDDA In the stove.

GEORGE Oh God, no, Hedda!

HEDDA The maid'll hear you.

GEORGE You burned Loevborg's amazing manuscript?

HEDDA I did.

GEORGE But that's a criminal act, Hedda. An immoral act, too. My gentle Hedda couldn't do something as immoral as that, could she?

HEDDA Listen to me. You came home from the judge's party this morning; and you told me Eilert had read to you alone for a full hour in the judge's breakfast room; and you said you thought it was the most amazing book you'd ever read; and you said you suddenly knew you were jealous of Eilert Loevborg because you felt it was very unfair that this weak and damaged man should be given that great talent —

GEORGE I know — I know — I know I said all that. But if I said I was jealous I didn't for a second mean that —

HEDDA So I burned the manuscript because I couldn't allow anyone to overshadow you.

GEORGE You burned the — ?

HEDDA I did it for you, George.

GEORGE For me?

HEDDA How could that be an immoral act?

GEORGE Oh my God . . .

HEDDA I did it for you, George. Believe me. For my husband.

Long pause.

GEORGE (*Almost whispers, in awe*) That you love me so profoundly, Hedda, I never knew that . . . never ever . . . no idea . . . none whatever . . . What an astonishing, what a humbling revelation . . . For my sake . . . My goodness, what can I say? . . . Oh my goodness, I'm speechless, love . . .

HEDDA (*Recklessly, wildly*) And now to fill your cup to over-
flowing. In four months' time — all being well, as
the quaint expression has it — all being well I'm
going to have a — No, no, no, no, no. Tell you what.
I'll get prescient Auntie Juju to spell it out for you.
She has known almost as long as I have.

Pause.

GEORGE In four months' time you're going to have — ?
You're not serious, Hedda!
HEDDA Yes.
GEORGE You really believe that in four months' time — all
being well — ? You really are serious, aren't you?
HEDDA Deadly.
GEORGE Wishful thinking. Trust me. That's what that is.
You're so eager, so desperately keen, your judge-
ment is clouded and you've convinced yourself it
really is happening. But it's not, Hedda, my love.
Believe me. Be sensible, darling — just isn't true.
(*Brief pause. He gazes at her*) Yes, it is! It is, isn't it?
Oh my God, yes, it's true! You know very well,
don't you? Yes, it is true! I mean, women have this
amazing intuitive sense about all kinds of things
and they're so often accurate, aren't they? Oh yes,
yes, yes, you know for certain — not a second of
doubt — that in four months — all being very, very
well — you're going to have a —
HEDDA (*Bitterly*) For God's sake, man!

Pause. GEORGE *is stunned. He drops on to a chair.*

GEORGE Oh, Hedda, my illustrious queen, this must be the
happiest moment of my entire . . .

*Pause. Silence. Then the three things — that she
burned the manuscript, that she burned the manuscript for him, that she is pregnant — all three col-
lide in his head and detonate. Now he is suddenly*

89

released — propelled — hurled into exaggerated, manic activity. He takes her hand, kisses it a dozen times, strokes his face with it and then returns it formally to her lap. He drops on his knees and salaams before her. He grabs a bundle of flowers and presents them to her. He takes several blooms and wreaths his head with them. He runs up to the back room, plays a few seconds of 'Chopsticks', runs back to the drawing room. He runs — dances — round the table, beating out a tattoo on it with his hands. During all this extravaganza HEDDA *sits absolutely still, rigid, upright, her eyes closed tight, her face a mask.*

Throughout his buffoonery GEORGE *pours out this commentary at top speed:*

GEORGE It will be a boy — and such a handsome boy he'll be! Congratulations, Hedda darling! We'll call him George the Second. No, we won't. We'll call him Joachim after his grandfather. Handsome Joachim the Second. Do you agree? Great!

But it may be a girl. And what an exquisite girl she'll be! Congratulations, Hedda darling! And we'll call her Hedda, won't we? Another celestial Hedda Tesman that will make this world even more numinous. No! Can't be Hedda! There can be only one Hedda, the unique Hedda who loves her husband inordinately. Juliana, then. No, no, no, not Juliana. Rena! Yes, exquisite Rena Tesman! Yes, that's a brilliant decision. Well done, Hedda! And we'll not make the announcement until after the funeral. We'll tell Auntie Juju first and then we'll tell Bertha. Bertha will be so delighted. Hold on — what about Bertha for a name! Now that's a thought! Wouldn't she be thrilled! No, no; don't jump about; stop changing your mind. Stick with Rena. Although it would give Bertha such a lift! Bertha Tesman! No. Maybe not this time. Next time maybe.

And we'll have to tell Thea Elvsted, dedicated-

to-her-anxieties Thea. I know you have reserva-
tions about her, Hedda. But she's a very good-
hearted woman and I know she will rejoice with
us. And Judge Brack of course. 'What splendid
news, Tesman! As the Americans have it — gee-
whiz.' And what about Eilert Loevborg? No, we'll
not tell Eilert; not yet anyway. I don't know why
but somehow it doesn't seem appropriate to tell
Eilert. And which room will be the nursery? I'll
leave that decision to you. And I'll use the other
room for my library. And riding lessons! Put their
names down immediately. They're bound to be
natural horse-people like their mother and their
grandfather, the General. And piano lessons! You
wouldn't want to take on that job. No, no, much
too boring. I'm told a young teacher has just set
up shop two doors down from the Planetarium.
They say she's very enthusiastic. I'll have a word
with her next week. They'll be superb pianists! My
goodness . . . oh my goodness . . .

> *He suddenly collapses on to the couch. He covers his
> face with his hands and lies there perfectly still and
> silent for five seconds.*

HEDDA (*Still rigid, eyes closed tight, body erect*) Oh God . . .
dear God . . . oh dear God . . .

> *Suddenly* GEORGE *is galvanized again. He leaps to
> his feet and resumes his buffoonery.*

GEORGE And slippers, Hedda! Slippers, slippers, embroi-
dered slippers! On their very first birthday and on
every birthday afterwards I'll embroider a wild
flower on their slippers, Joachim's and Rena's. I
can't embroider — but I'll learn. Isn't that a good
idea? Traditions must be maintained. (*He is suddenly calm and quiet again and speaks softly and slowly*)
Oh yes, oh yes, absolutely . . . this must be the

happiest moment of my entire . . .

HEDDA (*As before*) Will you tell Auntie Juju?

GEORGE She'll be the very first to know.

HEDDA That I burned Eilert's book?

She now opens her eyes and gazes at GEORGE.

GEORGE No, no, not that. She must never know that, Hedda. But what I would very much like her to know is that you did it for my sake. Maybe being pregnant, Hedda darling, perhaps that's what gave you the determination, did it? Or perhaps all young brides are as audacious on their husband's behalf as you?

HEDDA Ask your auntie that, too. Won't she know?

GEORGE (*Laughs uneasily*) I don't think she would, Hedda. She's a single girl after all. (*Suddenly miserable*) All the same, Eilert's manuscript — terrible, just terrible. That is a real catastrophe. Can't even begin to think about that.

THEA, *very agitated, rushes in from the hall.*

HEDDA Thea!

THEA I'm sorry — I'm back — forgive me.

HEDDA What's wrong, Thea?

GEORGE It's Eilert!

THEA Something has happened to him, Hedda.

GEORGE (*To* HEDDA) I told you, didn't I?

HEDDA Stop fidgeting. What has happened?

THEA I don't know. An accident of some sort, I think. When I got back to my lodgings they were whispering about him. Nobody seemed to know anything for sure. There were rumours of all sorts about what happened last night.

GEORGE That's all they are — rumours. I was with him last night. He went straight home to bed.

HEDDA What rumours?

THEA Something about a brawl — and the police being called — and a gun being fired. He's in the hospital, it seems.

HEDDA Nonsense.

GEORGE Oh my God . . .

THEA I went to his lodgings to find out what I could but they wouldn't even speak to me there.

GEORGE I'm going to the police — to the hospital. Eilert's in serious trouble. I told you that, Hedda, didn't I?

HEDDA You're going nowhere.

GEORGE I have got to —

HEDDA Keep out of this. This has nothing to do with you, nothing at all.

JUDGE BRACK *enters, looking very serious.*

GEORGE Judge Brack!

BRACK I had to see you. (*To* GEORGE) My condolences on your aunt, Tesman.

GEORGE Thank you.

BRACK (*To* HEDDA) And to you, madam.

HEDDA *bows.*

She was a gentle lady. I'll call on Miss Juliana later.

GEORGE Take a seat, Judge.

BRACK I'm here about another matter altogether.

THEA Eilert!

BRACK You know already, Mrs Elvsted?

THEA I've heard rumours, that's all.

BRACK Yes, it's Loevborg.

GEORGE (*To* HEDDA) See? (*To* BRACK) For God's sake, tell us!

BRACK *shrugs.*

BRACK Loevborg has been taken to hospital. He doesn't have long.

THEA Oh God, no — oh God . . .

HEDDA So soon?

THEA (*Beginning to cry*) And we parted in anger when I saw him last, Hedda.

HEDDA	Quiet.
THEA	I must go to him. I've got to see him before he dies.
BRACK	No point, Mrs Elvsted. They aren't allowing any visitors.
THEA	Tell me what happened.
GEORGE	But he — I mean — he didn't do it to himself, did he?
HEDDA	Of course he did.
GEORGE	Hedda!
BRACK	Mrs Tesman's assumption is correct.
THEA	Oh my God . . .
GEORGE	Suicide then?
HEDDA	Shot himself.
BRACK	Correct.
GEORGE	Good God!
BRACK	This afternoon. Between three and four, they think.
GEORGE	In his lodgings?
BRACK	(*Momentarily confused*) In his lodgings? — yes — I imagine yes —
THEA	That can't be right. I saw him later than four.
BRACK	Whenever then. I haven't got the details. All I know is that he shot himself in the chest.
THEA	Eilert Loevborg shouldn't have died like that. Dear, dear God . . .
HEDDA	(*To* BRACK) In the chest?
BRACK	According to the police.
HEDDA	Not in the temple?
BRACK	I was told the chest.
HEDDA	The heart. Not inappropriate.
BRACK	What do you mean?

HEDDA *turns away.*

GEORGE	And it's a bad wound?
BRACK	He may be dead already.
THEA	The judge is right. I know in my heart it's all over. Oh Hedda, Hedda . . .
HEDDA	How do you know all this?
BRACK	The police told me.

HEDDA	Thank heaven — at last something accomplished consciously.
GEORGE	What do you mean?
HEDDA	And achieved with beauty.
GEORGE	For God's sake, Hedda!
THEA	What's beautiful about it?
HEDDA	He settled his account with life after a lot of consideration and with a lot of fortitude.
THEA	I don't understand what she's saying.
HEDDA	And he settled with the style I expected from Eilert Loevborg. Yes, all that was appropriate; all that has a beauty.
THEA	Rubbish. He shot himself because he was a weak creature and because he was in despair.
GEORGE	Thea's right. I remember, even as a student, he used to have terrible stretches of depression.
THEA	Don't I know my Eilert? Some dark impulse took possession of him, just as he must have been possessed when he tore up our manuscript.
GEORGE	Thea's right.
HEDDA	I know Thea's wrong.
BRACK	Tearing up the manuscript — when did that happen?
THEA	Last night.
BRACK	Remarkable.
GEORGE	I just can't believe that the brilliant Eilert Loevborg would end it all like this and not make sure that the 'authentic thing', the 'genuine article' that would have immortalized him — that that was all secure. He knew it was his *succès d'estime*.
THEA	If only it could be pieced together again.
GEORGE	I'd give anything in the world for that.
THEA	It might be possible. What do you think?
GEORGE	I don't see how.
THEA	I think it just might. I kept all the notes he used to dictate from. I took them with me when I left home.

She searches through her bag and produces sheets of paper.

There. You're right — it's hopeless.

She hands the papers to GEORGE.

GEORGE You kept them all?

THEA They're a mess, I'm afraid.

GEORGE Maybe if they could be put in some sort of order . . . You know exactly what there is here?

THEA What do you think?

GEORGE Maybe . . .

THEA All I know is that nothing's missing.

GEORGE Maybe we can, Thea. Yes, I believe maybe we can.

THEA Do you?

GEORGE Yes, yes, yes, for Eilert's sake. We'll do it for him. I'll give over a year to it — two if I have to. For Eilert's sake.

HEDDA A very moral decision, George.

GEORGE He was my friend.

HEDDA Ah.

GEORGE If it's to be done it must be done in an organized fashion. There must be nothing sentimental about it.

THEA You're so right.

GEORGE Let's first see what we have. Where will we sit? Let's go into the back room. Will you excuse us?

THEA I think we can do it, Hedda. I know we can.

HEDDA Good for you, little Miss Rysing.

> GEORGE *and* THEA *go up to the back room. They sit at the table with their backs to* HEDDA *and* BRACK. *They begin sorting out the papers.*

There's such a sense of release in what Loevborg has done.

BRACK He must have thought so.

HEDDA I'm talking about *me*! The satisfaction in knowing that a destiny *can* be moulded; that you *can* nudge a man to achieve something daring and beautiful.

BRACK (*Smiling*) Influencing destinies is far beyond my

modest ambitions.

HEDDA (*Sharply*) You don't have to proclaim that, Judge. At heart you're just a commonplace bourgeois. Even your precious affectations can't disguise that.

BRACK And the bourgeois in me suspects Eilert Loevborg meant more to you than you like to admit. Am I right?

HEDDA I'm not in the stand. I've said all I'm going to say about Eilert Loevborg's final accomplishment. It had symmetry. It had grace. It was a triumph. Yes, Judge Brack, that destiny was important to me.

BRACK And for that reason I'm hesitant to shatter your illusions, dear Hedda. The record of events I adduced was incomplete — for Mrs Elvsted's sake. He was still alive when they rushed him to the hospital. He died within an hour. He never regained consciousness. And he didn't shoot himself in his lodgings.

HEDDA (*Impatiently*) So — so — so?

BRACK And it wasn't 'achieved' deliberately. Almost certainly an accident.

HEDDA Nonsense.

BRACK And in the boudoir of the cruelty-to-animals lady — what's her name? — the closet classicist — the artillery expert —

HEDDA (*Impatiently*) Where? — where? — who? —

BRACK Mademoiselle Circe!

HEDDA That's a lie! In her bedroom?

BRACK Where he spent the entire afternoon. Drunk, of course. He had gone back there to fetch something he claims she had taken from him.

HEDDA How drunk?

BRACK Blotto. Talked a lot of gibberish about a lost child. I supposed he meant his manuscript but Mrs Elvsted tells me he destroyed that himself. Perhaps his wallet then. Anyhow that's where he was found; in Circe's bedroom; with a discharged pistol in his breast pocket; blood pumping from a wound where he was — as they say . . . plugged?

HEDDA But in the heart?

BRACK Not the heart.

He points to his groin.

HEDDA Oh God . . . !

BRACK And one further disagreeable detail: the police suspect the pistol was stolen.

HEDDA Another lie! He didn't steal it! I —

BRACK (*Rapidly, softly*) Don't be so stupid, Hedda. It must have been stolen. The other explanation is . . . unthinkable.

GEORGE *and* THEA *come down from the other room. Their hands are filled with papers.*

GEORGE The light up there is poor and we need more space to spread the stuff out. May we use your desk, too?

HEDDA By all means. Hold on — let me tidy it.

GEORGE It's fine.

HEDDA I said I'll tidy it. You don't need this stuff.

She takes the revolver case from the drawer, covers it with sheets of music and goes up to the back room and off to the left — taking the revolver case with her. GEORGE *and* THEA *begin working at the table. They also use the desk for filing.*

GEORGE (*To* THEA) The first thing we must do is try to establish the date of each of these pages. Otherwise we'll never get them into sequence.

THEA I don't think they're all dated.

GEORGE What's that?

THEA April 7.

GEORGE And that?

THEA July 19.

GEORGE It *is* a mess.

HEDDA *returns. She stands behind* THEA *and runs her fingers through her hair.*

HEDDA   And how is the Loevborg memorial coming along?

THEA   (*Unhappily*) Hard to say, Hedda. The stuff's in chaos.

HEDDA   I have no doubt you're the woman to impose order on it — in your own diffident way.

GEORGE   It isn't going to be easy, but I believe we'll pull something together. As you know, Hedda, I'm first rate at cataloguing documents.

> HEDDA *sits on the footstool.* BRACK *stands behind her. They speak softly.*

HEDDA   And the police think the pistol was stolen?

BRACK   Softly, if you would. Let's assume he stole it from here. He was here this morning, was he not? There are witnesses — not least the redoubtable Bertha. Then you and he were alone here together; and at some point, perhaps, you left him by himself for a few minutes — perhaps you went looking for Bertha or perhaps there was somebody at the door. Anyhow he was left by himself. Where were the pistols?

HEDDA   Locked in that —

> *She breaks off suddenly. They exchange looks.*

BRACK   They weren't locked, were they?

HEDDA   You're right. They were lying on the table.

BRACK   Much more likely. And have you looked to see if both pistols are still there? Why trouble? I saw the pistol in the police station and I recognized it from yesterday — (*He mimes*) 'Bang-bang. It's only a game' — that one. Anyhow, the police have that gun now and are endeavouring to trace the owner.

HEDDA   Will they succeed?

BRACK   (*Leaning down to her ear and whispering*) Not as long as I keep mum.

HEDDA   Will you?

BRACK   At keeping mum I'm masterly. In fact I can't recall ever being a . . . snitch. Is that the noun?

HEDDA   And if you don't keep mum?

BRACK   You could always tell them he stole it.

HEDDA   I'd rather die.

BRACK   (*Smiling*) People say that, beautiful Hedda. It is estimable and they mean it. But they never do it.

HEDDA   And if they should trace the owner?

BRACK   Oh, then there'd be an enormous scandal — the type of scandal you have such a horror of. A court case, of course — you and classical Circe playing leading roles. She will tell us all how it happened. Was it an accident or was it manslaughter? Perhaps he was threatening her? Did the pistol go off as he pulled it from his jacket? Or did Miss Circe pull the pistol from him, shoot him and return the gun to his pocket? That would be in character. And as the case progresses, Mrs Tesman, you're certain to be asked the key question: Did you give him the pistol? And if it were to emerge that you did give it to him, what conclusions will people draw from that?

   But of course you're in no danger whatever as long as I don't snitch — may I employ the word as a verb?

HEDDA   I'm altogether in your power then?

BRACK   Hedda, darling —

HEDDA   Forever?

BRACK   You don't think for a second I'd abuse that position?

HEDDA   But you'd own me! (*She jumps up*) No, Judge, no! That won't happen!

BRACK   People can learn to live with what they can't change, Hedda Tesman.

HEDDA   Hedda Gabler can't, Judge Brack.

   She goes to the table where GEORGE *and* THEA *are working.*

   (*Forces cheeriness*) I have a sense things are going very well here.

GEORGE   Too early to say. All I know is it's going to be an enormous task — *if* we can do it.

HEDDA   It must feel a little strange for you, Thea, working beside George the way you did with Eilert Loevborg.

THEA   I suppose it is — yes.

HEDDA   But a new collaborator — there's an excitement in that, surely?

THEA   A great excitement. Imagine if I could inspire him too.

HEDDA   I believe you will. Give it time, Thea. Then step by step. Remember?

GEORGE   You're being facetious, darling, but I am aware of a . . . something in the atmosphere.

HEDDA   (*To* THEA) There!

GEORGE   I am — really!

HEDDA   It's called inspiration, George. Don't funk the word. Is funk acceptable, Judge?

BRACK   Perfectly. And interestingly, of English origin, not American.

GEORGE   Inspiration or whatever, you're interrupting it. Off you go and chat to the judge.

BRACK   Oxford slang actually. Eighteenth century.

HEDDA   So I'm of no use to you two soul-mates?

GEORGE   Will you please entertain my wife for me, Judge Brack?

BRACK   Nothing would pleasure me more.

HEDDA   I'm suddenly very tired. Would you mind if I lay down on the sofa for a while?

BRACK   Not in the least.

HEDDA   Just a short nap.

She goes up to the back room and pulls the curtains behind her.

GEORGE   (*To* THEA) I can't read his handwriting. There's a date scribbled there — what is it?

THEA   Either October the sixth or the eighth. It's the sixth.

Suddenly HEDDA *begins playing a wild, near-manic dance on the piano.*

THEA What's — ?

GEORGE (*Leaping to his feet*) Please, Hedda, darling! For heaven's sake! Not tonight! Think of Auntie Rena! And Eilert! Please!

The music stops. GEORGE *sits down again.* HEDDA *puts her head out through the curtains.*

HEDDA You're so right . . . thoughtless . . . forgive me . . . So from now on . . .

She puts her index finger to her lips and utters a 'Shhhhh' that goes on for a very, very long time. She withdraws again, closing the curtain behind her.

GEORGE She *is* tired. And very upset. And then us sitting here and working with Eilert's material, maybe that's a little insensitive, is it?

THEA We're all tired. It has been a long day.

GEORGE There's a thought, Thea. You could move in with Auntie Juju — Rena's room is empty now; and I could join you there every evening. We could work in peace there and we wouldn't annoy anybody.

THEA Would Miss Juliana agree?

HEDDA (*Off*) I hear every word you're saying. What will I do alone here every evening?

GEORGE Could the judge be coaxed into keeping you company?

BRACK (*To* GEORGE) You make it sound like a chore. (*To* HEDDA) It would be a most special delectation.

HEDDA (*Off*) Yes, you'd love that, Judge, wouldn't you? The only rooster in the yard.

BRACK (*Musing to himself*) The only rooster in the yard . . . The only bull in the pen . . . The only cock on the dunghill . . . Why does it have to be so farmyard? Why not the only orchid in the conservatory? The only butterfly in the wheatfield? The only lark in the prairie?

A sudden shot, off. All leap to their feet.

GEORGE She's playing with those damned pistols again! For
      God's sake, Hedda . . . !

      BERTHA *rushes in.*

BERTHA Did I hear a — ?

      GEORGE *flings the curtains back and rushes into*
      the back room. THEA *follows him.* HEDDA *has shot*
      herself in the head. She is lying on the sofa. There is
      blood everywhere.

GEORGE Hedda! Oh Jesus Christ! Oh Hedda! Jesus Christ!
  THEA Oh my God!
BERTHA No, no, no — please — please — no, no.
GEORGE (*In total shock*) She has shot herself in the temple,
      Judge Brack.
  BRACK (*Refusing to hear*) Can't hear what the man's saying.
  THEA Oh my God, George . . .
  BRACK What are you saying, Tesman?
GEORGE She has shot herself in the temple, Judge Brack.
  BRACK That's a damned lie!
BERTHA God forgive the poor unhappy creature.
  THEA George . . . George . . .
BERTHA May God in his mercy overlook all her human
      faults.
GEORGE She has killed herself, Judge Brack, and handsome
      young Joachim or maybe exquisite young Rena,
      Judge Brack.
  BRACK Never! I will not have that!
GEORGE In the temple, Judge Brack.
  BRACK That's a damned lie! For God's sake, reasonable
      people just don't do things like that.

      Fade to black.